THE WORDS OF A GENTLEMAN

"You are a remarkable young woman, Miss Sterling. The qualities you prized in your young man—the qualities you discovered he does not possess—speak very well for the kind of person you are."

"I am overcome by your approval," she said dryly. "I only wish I could have come by it in an easier manner."

To her surprise, Westbrook, who had pulled his chair around to face her, took both her hands in his and pulled her closer to him, so their faces were very near.

"I grant you, Miss Sterling, I am neither a handsome man nor a charming one, nor am I daring enough to wish to go away to war, but the other characteristics you named I believe I do possess."

Thrown completely off guard by his unexpected behavior, Ivy thought frantically for a response. With relief, she seized upon one.

"Loyalty to those you care for?" she asked, raising her brows. "I believe, sir, you told me you do not care for others."

"Loyalty to those I care for?" he repeated, inching closer. "That would be to you, Miss Sterling, for I am very much afraid I do care for you." Here he pulled her to him and kissed her soundly. . . .

Books by Mona Gedney

A LADY OF FORTUNE

THE EASTER CHARADE

A VALENTINE'S DAY GAMBIT

A CHRISTMAS BETROTHAL

A SCANDALOUS CHARADE

A DANGEROUS AFFAIR

A LADY OF QUALITY

A DANGEROUS ARRANGEMENT

MERRY'S CHRISTMAS

LADY DIANA'S DARING DEED

LADY HILARY'S HALLOWEEN

AN ICY AFFAIR

Published by Zebra Books

AN ICY AFFAIR

Mona Gedney

ZEBRA BOOKS
Kensington Publishing Corp.
http://www.kensingtonbooks.com

ZEBRA BOOKS are published by

Kensington Publishing Corp.
850 Third Avenue
New York, NY 10022

All Kensington titles, imprints and distributed lines are
available at special quantity discounts for bulk purchases for
sales promotion, premiums, fund-raising, educational or
institutional use.

Special book excerpts or customized printings can also be
created to fit specific needs. For details, write or phone the
office of the Kensington Special Sales Manager: Kensington
Publishing Corp., 850 Third Avenue, New York, NY 10022.
Attn. Special Sales Department. Phone: 1-800-221-2647.

Zebra and the Z logo Reg. U.S. Pat. & TM Off.

First Printing: October 2002
10 9 8 7 6 5 4 3 2 1

Printed in the United States of America

One

"I *shall* go to London!" Ivy exclaimed, clenching her fists and glaring at her uncle. "It is my right to have a coming out, and you are my guardian! It is your duty to provide me with one instead of keeping me trapped in this godforsaken place!"

Her cheeks were almost as crimson as her gown, and with some difficulty she kept herself from flinging the book she had been reading at her uncle's head. He was, she felt, the most unbearable of men. She was accustomed to thinking herself a person of importance, but her uncle clearly disagreed. Her wishes mattered not at all to him.

Alistair Sterling shrugged, tapping slender fingers idly upon a polished tabletop as he stared out the frosted window at the thickly falling snow. His niece might as well have been making some casual observation about the weather for all the attention he gave her comment.

"I have not the slightest intention either of going to London myself or of sending you," he returned coolly, staring over her head as he spoke. "Your coming out is of no consequence to me. The whole process is, in fact, a nonsensical tradition, a waste of money and a waste of time. It makes silly girls even sillier than they are. You shall marry in good time— when I find you a suitable husband."

Ivy was still glaring at him, but before she could respond, he had turned and strolled from the room without having shown the slightest trace of emotion, his gray eyes as frozen as the pond in the garden. She shook with fury, pounding one small fist into her palm. What she had done to earn her uncle's dislike she had not the slightest notion, but his distaste for her was all too obvious.

He seldom made eye contact with her, and in the ten months since her parents' deaths, he had treated her as a stranger who happened to be sharing a roof with him, never calling her by name, never speaking of her parents. Unless she sought him out—something she did only when absolutely necessary—she seldom saw him during the course of a day. Indeed, for a good portion of the months she had lived at Foxridge Hall, he had been gone, leaving her to the care of her governess. There had been some comfort in that at first, for the two of them had grieved together over the loss of her parents, and her governess at least provided a measure of warmth and companionship. Alistair Sterling, on the other hand, showed no interest in her or her loss. He appeared to feel he had done all that was required of him by providing her with food, clothing, and shelter.

Finally even the faithful Miss Willowby had abandoned Ivy when Miss Willowby had received a letter from her own elderly mother asking for help while she recovered from a fever. Ivy did not blame her governess for leaving. The loneliness of their situation had become too oppressive. They saw no one else except the servants, and their only outings were to a nearby village, which boasted a tea shop and a lending library.

After Miss Willowby's departure, Ivy and MacTavish, her small black terrier, had been left completely to themselves. Alistair Sterling had behaved as though nothing had changed, however, leaving his niece to fend for herself. For two months, Ivy had been left with no one to talk to except MacTavish and the servants, and during that time she had become determined to force him to take her to London so that she could take her place in society. She was aware her parents had left her in comfortable circumstances, but her uncle, unfortunately, held the purse strings and made the decisions. She knew it had never occurred to her parents that she might lose both of them at once and be placed with this relative she had never met.

Ivy watched the door close behind him, infuriated by her helplessness. Then, careless of the weather or of anything except her own anger, she plunged out a side door with MacTavish at her heels, avoiding the inevitable footman at the entrance to the Hall. Just why her uncle had one stationed there was beyond her, she thought for the thousandth time, raising her arm to protect her face from the snow that swirled about her. Her uncle's house might as well be located at some far corner of the world, for not once since she had lived there had anyone come to see them.

She had never lived in such solitude when her parents were alive. Lawrence and Gwendolyn Sterling had been a happy, lively couple, and their only child had been taken with them everywhere, not consigned to the nursery as most children were. The shock of losing them had been great, but the shock of her present situation had been greater still.

Ivy had never met her uncle while her parents were living, nor had he been present for their funeral service. Nonetheless, her parents' solicitor had explained to her that she was to move to her uncle's home, for he was her only living relative.

When she and Miss Willowby had arrived at Foxridge Hall, exhausted by the journey and the painful events of the past weeks, he had shown no more interest in her than he would have in a new servant—perhaps less, in fact. She and her governess were comfortably housed and fed, and Miss Willowby was able to order whatever books or clothing Ivy required, but the two of them dined alone in the schoolroom, a place Ivy hated. In fact, the only place where she was happy was the old gatehouse, now deserted since the last gatekeeper had died some two years earlier. She went there often to watch the coaches and tilburies and carts go by her on the high road beyond the wall, reassuring her that there was still a real world beyond the walls of Foxridge Hall.

Her governess, however, had felt she should not

go there unchaperoned, and so Ivy's activities had been circumscribed. She had not even been able to ride, for Miss Willowby, who did not ride herself, had insisted she be attended by a groom. Alistair Sterling had informed her he had none to spare, looking over her head as he always did when forced to speak to her. She could not recall a single time when they had made eye contact.

After Miss Willowby's departure, Ivy was free to go to the gatehouse whenever she wished, for her uncle paid no attention to her. Starved for activity, she went there regularly and perched on the stone wall beside it, watching eagerly for the occasional coach or carriage or rider to go by. Even passing carts offered some glimpse of the outside world. Inside the gatehouse, which was still furnished, though sparsely, she had established her own hideaway, with a small supply of food and her favorite books. There was a healthy stock of firewood left by the last gatekeeper, and she occasionally treated herself and MacTavish to the comfort of a crackling fire. While there, she could pretend all was right with her world.

Thinking of that comfort now, Ivy hurried as quickly as she could through the cold, her head bent against the heavy snow and her small terrier trotting closely behind her. Now, she thought miserably, now she was truly alone, for Miss Willowby was gone, promising she would come back when she could, when her mother had recovered from the illness that had overtaken her—but Ivy knew better. Foxridge Hall had oppressed her governess as much as it did Ivy, and she was certain Miss Wil-

lowby had no intention of returning. Except for
MacTavish, Ivy now had no one who cared a far-
thing about her.

When this bleak truth had dawned upon her, she
had decided she, too, would leave. After all, she
had had her seventeenth birthday, and she was
ready to make her entrance into society, as her
mother had planned. She was determined Alistair
Sterling was not going to prevent it. He had no
such right, whether he was her guardian or not!

The heat of her anger had kept her warm for a
few minutes, but suddenly Ivy realized she was shivering and her teeth were chattering. Her red
muslin gown and thin-soled sandals offered no protection against the biting cold, and she regretted
the hasty fit of temper that had sent her running
headlong from the hall without benefit of cloak or
sturdy boots. She had paid no attention to the
weather, and the snow that had begun so suddenly
was now ankle deep and falling more thickly, the
wind flinging it in her face and whirling it around
her until she soon was lost in a whirlpool of white.

Stopping to call for MacTavish, she was relieved
to find him still close behind her. "Good boy!" she
said gratefully, running her hands over his snowy
coat and rubbing his muzzle between her palms.
He gave a sudden, sharp bark in response, and she
grinned. "I thought I could run directly to the gatehouse, Mac, but I think we're out of luck. No fire
for us today," she continued ruefully, standing up
and trying to get her bearings. "We'll be lucky to
find our way back to the Hall."

Running out in such a fashion had been a hen-witted thing to do, she knew. She was already shaking with cold as she tried to get her bearings, but she was determined to remain calm. It was not as though she had any place to run to except the dratted gatehouse. The one comfort was that since her uncle had no interest in her, she would not have to account for her foolish actions when she returned. Carefully, she looked around to try to identify a landmark. At the moment she was no longer certain that she was on the drive to the Hall, or that she was even moving in the proper direction to reach the road. The huge flakes of damp snow were sticking to everything and piling up at an alarming rate. The wind was already driving it into drifts, and nothing appeared normal.

Then she realized the question was not when she would return to the Hall but whether she could manage to do so at all. Although she knew she could have not gone far and she thought she had indeed been walking down the drive at least part of the time, the thick snow that frosted her eyelashes revealed only a landscape that had turned into an unfamiliar blur of white.

Suddenly she slipped and pitched sideways, the leather soles of her slippers grown too slick in the damp snow, but before she could scramble to her feet, MacTavish uttered a volley of sharp staccato barks and raced by her. Ivy heard a startled whinny, accompanied by the muffled thudding of hooves, and she screamed, rolling away from the sound and coating herself with snow.

"What the devil?" came an angry voice. "Who's there?"

"Ivy Sterling!" she cried. "Who are you?"

"And what do you have with you?" the voice demanded, ignoring her question. "Muzzle that beast before he oversets my horse!"

Indignant at his tone, Ivy struggled to her feet and glared in the direction of the voice. "Come here, MacTavish! Good boy!"

"Don't tell the damned little beast he's a good boy when he's caused such a furor! Damn near caused me to be pitched off!"

Suddenly a dark form appeared through the curtain of snow, and the rider swung down from the saddle and took a step toward her. "What do you do? Train the little beggar to attack hapless travelers?"

She could dimly see the speaker now, but that was scarcely comforting, she thought. He was a dark, sturdy man, and he carried his riding crop as though he knew how to use it.

"I trust you don't plan to use that!" she snapped, a sudden rush of anger helping to warm her and keep her teeth from chattering. "And as for being a hapless traveler, you're no longer on a public road! You chose to enter our gates and you're now inside the walls of Foxridge Hall, sir!"

"Am I indeed?" he replied, clearly unimpressed. "Well, I've never heard of the place, but I'm happy to know it is here, nonetheless. I can't possibly keep on riding in this weather. Kindly direct me to the Hall."

"Naturally," she replied, attempting to bob a

mock curtsey in spite of the fact that she was shaking with the cold. "I should be happy to run ahead and guide you as though I were some common stableboy, sir—if I had the slightest notion in which direction I should run."

The intruder squinted through the snow at her, bringing his face uncomfortably close to hers. "Are you out here wandering around in a blizzard without any coat?" he asked abruptly. "What a bird-witted chit you must be!"

The fact that he pulled a woolen cloak from a saddlebag and wrapped it around her did nothing to allay the sting of his remark. However, her teeth were now rattling at such a rate that she was forced to wait to make a retort—and she certainly did not refuse the comfort of the cloak.

"Miss Sterling—I think that's what you said your name is—allow me," he said. Before she knew what was happening, he had swung her up to the saddle. "Hold on, ma'am, and your small beast and I—or at least the small beast—will lead you home."

He looked down at the terrier, who was regarding him suspiciously with sharp dark eyes. "Well?" said the gentleman, shaking his crop at the dog. "Go along! Go home, little beast!"

"Home, Mac. Take us home!" Ivy managed to croak. What a travesty it was to use that word about Foxridge Hall, she thought. Still, it was their only home now.

The dog's ears pricked up at her command, and he turned and started gingerly through the deepening snow, which the drifts now made deeper than his short legs. The stranger, reins in hand, strode after MacTavish, leading his mount carefully. Ivy huddled gratefully in the folds of the cloak and hoped her dog indeed knew where they were going. The little terrier had been her mainstay for years, so she felt that if it were possible to bring her to safety, MacTavish would do so.

The stranger's mount picked its way carefully through the rippling snow, and Ivy was grateful to feel herself firmly held in place. The man had no manners, to be sure, but he seemed to be an adequate horseman. At least she had some prospect of making it to safety.

A sudden vision of her uncle's face when confronted by the snow-covered, square-shouldered, irritated stranger made her chuckle unexpectedly. Alistair Sterling was about to have an unpleasant experience, and she looked forward to enjoying every moment of it. The dark figure walking beside her looked up sharply at the unexpected sound.

"I'm pleased you are enjoying yourself, Miss Sterling," he remarked dryly. "Your amusement seems a little ill-timed, however."

Warmer now in the wool cloak, Ivy was able to answer him briskly. "We entertain no visitors at Foxridge Hall, sir, so I was thinking of how pleased my uncle will be at your arrival."

Before he could respond, MacTavish announced their presence at the entrance to the Hall by scratching at the door and barking. The footman, shocked by such an unusual occurrence, threw it open abruptly, and the small dog trotted into the warmth, shaking himself violently to be rid of the damp, clinging snow. Behind him came two snow-covered figures, and the footman stood stock-still, stunned by the unexpected sight.

"Well, don't just stand there, you fool!" snapped the stranger. "Help her!"

Jolted into motion by a voice of authority, he bowed, finally recognizing his master's niece.

"Miss Sterling," he murmured, helping her into the hall and removing her cloak. Seeing the condition of her dress and slippers, he moved briskly to summon one of the maids to help her, then turned to the stranger.

"Damned dog and damned dolt of a footman!" said the man, throwing down his riding crop and shaking the snow off his top hat. He eyed Mac-Tavish with deep disfavor, a look completely lost upon the terrier, who was industriously rolling across an exquisite Aubusson carpet to dry himself.

Bowing and turning a deaf ear to the curses of the stranger, the footman helped him from his sodden greatcoat and watched the passageway hopefully. At any moment the butler, startled into unaccustomed activity by the ringing of the bell, should appear and take charge of this unheard-of situation. The footman, in the two years he had served at the Hall, had been called upon only twice to care for visitors.

"What the devil is all this?" demanded Alistair Sterling, staring out at the group from the doorway to his library.

"Exactly what I was thinking!" returned the stranger. "Why the devil am I not being welcomed into this house? Here I stand, a stranger, stranded by an ungodly storm, my poor blasted horse left standing in front of your door, and—" Pausing a moment, he waved a hand in Ivy's direction. "And there stands the daughter of the house, frozen to the bone, with no one to help her—"

"She is not my daughter!" responded Sterling abruptly. "She is my niece."

"And so I suppose it is quite acceptable for your niece to stand there freezing!" retorted the stranger. "And obviously it seems acceptable to you to offer no shelter to me and my horse!"

Stung, Sterling straightened his shoulders and glowered at the stranger. "Of course you shall have shelter!" Briskly, he gave orders to the footman to send a stableboy to take care of the stranger's mount. Then he turned back to the man, and bowed his head briefly. "My name is Alistair Sterling," he said. "And this is Foxridge Hall."

"So your niece informed me," said the stranger, bowing in return. "And I am Robert Westbrook of Grampton Hills, far to the north of here."

He paused a moment, then added stiffly, "I apologize for my poor manners. I fear being slowed by this damnable storm has made me short-tempered. I am on my way to London on vital business, and being stopped in such an unexpected way made me angry."

"Quite understandable," returned Sterling, his tone quite as stiff. "You are welcome here for as long as the storm holds. My butler will show you to a chamber."

Here he nodded toward Wheeling, the elderly butler, and turned to go back into his library, then paused and added, "And both of us will pray for better weather soon."

Westbrook gave a brief, abrupt laugh, and Ivy, catching a glimpse of her uncle's expression as he turned, chuckled to herself as she finished drying MacTavish in front of the fire with the towel the maid had brought her. How pleasing to see her uncle thrown off balance in such a manner, she thought in amusement. She found herself looking forward to the developments of the evening.

Wheeling, his expression still one of amazement at this unexpected occurrence, tottered toward the stairs, leading their guest to his chamber. Westbrook paused as he passed Ivy and nodded at her.

"Foxridge Hall is quite an impressive place, Miss Sterling," he said, his brows high as he glanced around the Great Hall, its whitewashed walls rising high above them, studded darkly with weaponry of bygone days. She knelt on the huge hearth, the best place for drying her dog immediately. "I can see why you are so proud of it."

"Proud of it?" she replied, startled. "Foxridge Hall is nothing to me."

He glanced at her, his dark winged brows growing closer together. "You told me pretty quickly where I was when we met."

Ivy shrugged, trying not to shiver. The maid had tried to take her upstairs to her chamber, but Ivy would not go up before drying MacTavish. "You were attempting to order us about, and I did not

take it well, sir. I merely wanted you to know you
were on private grounds."

"I see." He paused a moment longer, then said
abruptly, "You'd best get upstairs and take care of
yourself, ma'am. This place is filled with draughts
and you will catch your death the moment you
leave that fire."

"Thank you for your advice, sir," Ivy returned
tartly, gathering MacTavish up in a dry towel. "I
don't know how I should have managed without it."

A brief smile glimmered on Westbrook's face,
but Ivy missed it. "My very thought, Miss Sterling,"
he replied, bowing. "I have found my advice is generally helpful to lesser mortals."

Before she could reply indignantly, he had hurried up the stairs behind Wheeling.

"Insufferable man!!" she remarked to MacTavish,
whose tail twitched in agreement. "Indeed, we shall
pray the storm *is* soon over!"

Two

Ivy hurriedly washed in the can of hot water that the maid had brought for her, toweling dry her wet hair, which curled in dark determination around her face. Miss Willowby had often commented how grateful she should be to have no need of curling tongs in order to achieve the ringlets that were so fashionable. And at this particular moment, Ivy was grateful, for it saved her a great deal of time. She hastily caught the curls into a bunch at the top of her head, binding them with a scarlet ribbon and leaving a few loose around her face.

Eagerly she hurried down the stairway, anxious not to be deprived of any amusement their guest might offer. He might annoy her, but she was equally certain he would infuriate her uncle. She had had no entertainment for months, and she cared not at all if her uncle thought her behavior forward. She felt certain Robert Westbrook would give her uncle a shaking such he had not received during his days of living in seclusion at the Hall.

She and MacTavish once again took up residence close to the vast hearth in the Great Hall, carefully seating themselves behind a heavy tapestry screen that would shield them both from drafts and from inquiring eyes. The footman, once again at his post, looked neither left nor right, as he had been taught, so he did not acknowledge her presence. Her uncle, she knew, would still be safely secluded in the sanctuary of his library, and Mr. Westbrook, she hoped, would soon put in an appearance.

Soon enough she saw MacTavish's ears prick up, and then she heard the sound of Westbrook's boots on the wide oaken stairway that led into the Great Hall. The little dog started to rise, but Ivy caught him. "Just wait a moment, Mac," she whispered. "Let's see what happens."

Obediently, the little dog sank back down at her feet, and together they listened eagerly. She heard Westbrook pause at the foot of the stairs and demand of the footman, "Where is your master?"

Peeking from behind the screen, Ivy saw the footman bow and lead Mr. Westbrook toward the library. She smiled in anticipation. The household knew disturbing Mr. Sterling in the library was forbidden, but the footman was caught between two unhappy choices. He knew the stranger would curse at him if he declined to show him to the master, and he was uncertain now whether his master would curse him for showing in the guest or for failing to do so. His lot was not a happy one.

Poker-faced, he led Westbrook toward the library and announced him. Westbrook, not standing on ceremony, marched past the footman and entered the library.

"Well, Sterling," she heard him say, his deep voice resonating through the Hall, "have you any brandy worth the drinking? And when do we dine? Do you keep country hours? I must say I am famished after that hellish ride through the snow!"

Ivy could not hear her uncle's response, for Westbrook had slammed the door behind him. Amused at what she knew must be her uncle's consternation at this invasion of his privacy, she scratched Mac's ears and waited for an eruption from the library.

Before one could occur, however, there was a heavy knocking at the door. MacTavish stood foursquare and barked imperiously at this unaccustomed noise, and the footman bolted from the library to answer it. Her uncle and Mr. Westbrook also appeared at the doorway of the library, curious to see what the storm had brought.

Ivy knelt beside her pet and held his collar firmly. "Good boy," she whispered, "but be quiet." She closed his muzzle gently and tapped it with her finger.

When the footman opened the door, a gust of wind blew in two tall gentlemen, coated from hat to heel in snow and clutching their valises.

"Thank you! Thank you!" exclaimed the taller of them. "I had begun to think we were completely lost and I should never see a fire again!"

The fire in the Hall was blazing brightly, and the young man strode toward it gratefully, tossing aside his greatcoat and his hat, holding his hands toward its flames. Sighing gratefully, he ran long fingers through his hair, shaking the snow from it.

Ivy, watching from behind the screen, caught her breath. He was the most startlingly handsome young man she had ever seen, his hair the color of polished copper, his blue eyes merry.

Unfortunately, when she caught her breath, she released her hold on MacTavish's collar, and he bounded toward the guest, eager to inspect this newcomer for himself.

Ivy hurried after him and succeeded in catching him just before he launched himself toward the young man.

"I do beg your pardon, sir!" she exclaimed, scooping up her pet.

The young man stood perfectly still and stared at her for a moment, then caught himself and bowed. "I am honored, ma'am. If this is your dog, I declare myself ready to be mauled by him anytime you say the word."

Ivy's dimples deepened as she dropped a curtsey and smiled up at him through her eyelashes. The intensity of his gaze caught her off guard, and she quickly lowered her eyes and gave her attention to MacTavish.

"I fear MacTavish has no manners," she observed, rumpling the dog's fur affectionately.

"That, Miss Sterling, is an understatement," observed Mr. Westbrook abruptly. He had strolled over to join them at the fire. "You will find, sir," he said, looking at the newcomer, "that the little beast will do you in if he can manage it. Damn near caused me to be thrown from my mount."

Here he stared with dark disapproval at the terrier, and MacTavish, well aware he was being discussed, stared intently into Westbrook's eyes, his tail thumping steadily on the floor. Ivy was amused to see Westbrook look away first.

"That seems a bit harsh," said the second newcomer, who had joined them at the fire. "He looks to be quite a good little fellow."

"Oh, he is," agreed Ivy, grateful someone would say a word for her pet. "Some people have no appreciation of dogs," she added darkly, looking disapprovingly at Westbrook, who snorted.

"Well, I assure you, ma'am, my brother and I have the deepest appreciation of the canine world. We had a kennel filled with them when we were young," said the handsome young stranger, bowing to her again. "And forgive my poor breeding in not introducing myself. I am Edmund Montgomery, recently of Blayford, Cumberland, and this is my brother Randall, until just two days ago the rector of Little Ellis."

Westbrook glanced back at his host, who appeared to be taking no part in the proceedings. Feeling as though the manners were becoming a little too informal for a young female, he stepped forward without hesitation. Indeed, thought Ivy in irritation, he seemed to be a man who never hesitated.

"And I am Robert Westbrook, the gentleman standing at the door is Mr. Alistair Sterling, the master of the house, and this is Miss Sterling, his niece," he said, intervening between the two and bowing to Montgomery.

Ivy frowned at his presumptuousness, but the expression melted immediately when she saw Edmund

Montgomery's warm smile. He was, she thought, more personable than any of the many gentlemen she had met while traveling with her parents—and her experience had been wide.

"I am delighted to make your acquaintance, Miss Sterling," he said, patting MacTavish's head once more. "And that of MacTavish, of course," he added hastily. "I would not wish to affront your pet."

The terrier showed no sign of being affronted, accepting the rubbing between his ears with equanimity.

Here Randall Montgomery turned to Alistair Sterling. "We apologize for such an intrusion, sir," he said, "but I am afraid our coach can go no farther. We were forced to abandon it just inside your gate, and the driver has loosed the horses and led them back to your stables. He was fearful they would suffer permanent harm if he did not take them back directly. We do apologize for the intrusion."

Sterling spoke sharply to the footman. "Gerald! Make certain the horses and the driver are cared for, and notify Wheeling that we will have two more guests for the evening."

As the footman, looking overwhelmed by this development, started from the room, Edmund Montgomery called out cheerfully, "My brother and I will happily share a chamber!"

"There is no need of that," said Sterling abruptly. "I have no shortage of rooms."

"I daresay not," agreed Edmund. "This appears to be quite a venerable pile. No doubt you are accustomed to having scores of guests."

"No," said Sterling briefly. "I am not. Not since my parents' time have there been guests." Here he turned back to his library. "If you will excuse me, I must return to my work. Wheeling will show you to your chambers, and we will dine at seven. Please feel free to ask the servants for anything you require."

And he walked into the library and closed the door abruptly. The others glanced at each other in surprise, and Ivy flushed in embarrassment.

"As you can see, my uncle is not accustomed to company," she said apologetically. "He does not wish to be rude." In truth, she was quite certain he did not care one way or another about rudeness.

"It is no matter," Edmund hastened to assure her. "We are more than grateful to have shelter from this unexpected storm. He is kind to take us in."

At that point, Wheeling arrived to show the Montgomerys to their chambers, and as the footman gathered their luggage, Edmund turned once again to Ivy.

"I shall look forward to seeing you at dinner, Miss Sterling," he said, smiling down at her.

"I fear I shall not be at dinner," she said slowly, hating that she had to make her humiliation public. "I do not dine with my uncle."

"No?" inquired young Montgomery in surprise. Then he took her hand and bent over it, brushing it with his lips. "Perhaps we can do something about that, ma'am."

"That would be quite presumptuous of us," announced Westbrook firmly. "I am certain Mr. Sterling has a reason for this—and it would be unseemly for a young woman, not even out, to be in company at dinner with no other lady present."

"And how do you know I am not yet out, sir?" she demanded, glaring at him.

Westbrook glanced down at her heart-shaped face and wide, innocent eyes. Had he been capable of grinning, he might have done so. As it was, his expression lightened momentarily. He bowed and said gravely, "Shall we say it was just a fortunate guess, ma'am?"

He looked at her furious expression and asked gently, "And are you saying I am inaccurate, Miss Sterling? Have you indeed had your coming out? If that is so, I shall make my apology most handsomely, I assure you."

Infuriated by her inability to correct him, she made a brief bow to the Montgomery brothers, nodded in curt acknowledgement of Mr. Westbrook, and, rigid with anger, she marched toward the stairs, MacTavish in her arms.

By the time she reached her chamber, she was furious. "He had absolutely no reason to humiliate me in such a manner!" she told her dog, striding up and down the length of her room. MacTavish watched her alertly, his ears pricked forward, listening carefully to the tone of her voice.

"He clearly thinks far too well of himself—and he takes far too much upon himself!" she exclaimed, jerking loose the sashes that kept her drapes open. "It is quite insufferable that he should tell our guests I have not yet had my coming out and I should remain upstairs for my meals—quite insufferable!"

She punctuated her observation by picking up a china teacup to hurl at the wall. However, looking at it and holding its fragile beauty in her hand, she placed it gently down on its saucer on the tray. Then she turned to MacTavish and stamped her foot.

"It's completely unfair, Mac!" she exclaimed, throwing herself across her bed. "We shall be stuck up here by ourselves again. I didn't mind when there was nothing happening downstairs, but now that there is company, it is quite intolerable!"

MacTavish, his ears pricked and his attention caught by the distress in her voice, barked sharply in agreement.

Ivy giggled and hung her hand over the edge of the bed so the terrier could burrow his head into it. She was quite determined she would dine with the company. The only question now was just how to achieve it—and, of course, just what she should wear. The image of Mr. Edmund Montgomery's charming smile lingered in her mind.

"What do you think, Mac?" she inquired. "The brown merino with golden ribbons or the blue muslin trimmed with blue and white ribbons?"

They regarded one another seriously for a moment. Then she nodded. "You are quite right. It must be the blue."

And she set about preparing herself for the evening.

Three

Ivy had just reached the top of the stairway to the Great Hall when she once more heard a heavy pounding at the door. The library door flew open and her uncle appeared.

"Gerald, if there are more strangers in need of shelter, tell them to keep riding until they reach the village!"

"Nonsense, Uncle!" she said loudly, startling all three of them. "It is six miles and more to the village. They would never make it there in this storm. Open the door, Gerald!"

And Gerald opened the door, for the moment ignoring his master.

To their astonishment, Gerald opened the door not to one or two stranded travelers, but to a crowd of them. The newcomers rushed into the room with exclamations of relief. An icy wind tore at their hats and scarves and swept through the Great Hall. Even MacTavish was too surprised to bark, and Ivy snatched him up before he could rush downstairs. At first it was difficult for Ivy, leaning intently over the railing, to determine just how many there were.

Finally, she was able to make an approximate head-count. There were at least nine of them.

There was an inordinate amount of coughing, stamping, and exclaiming as they shook off the snow and looked about them. From their midst emerged a tall man in a greatcoat with more capes than she could count. He strode toward Alistair Sterling and bowed low to him.

"Our deepest gratitude, dear sir, for opening the doors of your home to us."

"Yes, but there's only one door that was opened, Reg, didn't you notice that?" spoke up a tall, thin man with a reedy voice. "And I'm certain the gentleman knows as how it was only the one door as was opened to us."

Ivy listened with amusement. The thin man was clearly inclined to be literal, and it was just as clear that "Reg" was outraged by this interruption. He threw the culprit a dark glance, and turned back to Sterling.

"As I was saying, dear sir, I am Reginald Ravensby, at your service. Because of the raging elements that have brought disaster upon us, I fear we must intrude upon your hospitality."

Ivy could see that her uncle was looking anything but hospitable. However, before he could respond, a second figure from the group approached him.

"What he means to say is that our driver ran the coach into a ditch, and I don't know what we would have done if we hadn't found your gate. Even then, it would have done us no good were it not for the lights shining from your windows. They served to guide us to your door, and for that we are most grateful."

The second speaker was a woman with a vibrant, gracious voice, and she drew close to Sterling and extended a gloved hand. To Ivy's surprise, her uncle took the woman's hand and bowed over it.

"I am grateful our lights guided you here to safety, ma'am," he said—a little stiffly, it was true, but more charitably than his niece had expected. "Do come close to the fire, ma'am, so you may warm yourself while a chamber is prepared for you. You look almost frozen by your adventure."

"How very kind you are, sir," she murmured, allowing him to lead her close to the blaze, the rest of the group trailing behind them, Ravensby and the literal young man hotly engaged in argument. "May I ask to whom we are indebted for such hospitality?"

"Forgive me, ma'am. I have been so long away from society that I have virtually forgotten its rules. I am Alistair Sterling, and you have found your way to Foxridge Hall."

He looked into her eyes as he led her closer to the fire, and Ivy leaned forward, watching him in disbelief. He appeared to be falling under this woman's spell more rapidly than she could have imagined possible.

"And it was our great good fortune to find our way to the door of such a generous man, sir," she said, smiling up at him. "My name is Divina Durrell, and this"—she waved her hand in the direction of the others, who were trying to crowd as closely as possible to the fire—"is my acting troupe. We were on our way to perform at a house party given by the Earl of Lakeside when we had our mishap on the road."

An actress! Ivy almost exclaimed it aloud, so delighted was she by the news. She studied Miss Durrell as carefully as she could from this distance. The actress had thrown back the hood of her cape so her chestnut hair glowed against the hood's dark velvet lining. Glancing at her uncle's face, she could see she was not the only one who thought Miss Durrell breathtaking.

"Now, Mr. Sterling, you must allow me to introduce you to the rest of *my* acting troupe," announced Reginald Ravensby, glaring at Miss Durrell, who regarded him blandly.

He took the hand of a young woman and pulled her forward, as though to take a bow at the end of a performance. "This is Miss Rosa Evans," he announced, his voice deep and highly theatrical. "She is as gifted as any actress who has ever trod the boards"—here he looked pointedly at Miss Durrell again—"and a more heartwrenching portrayal of Ophelia than hers you will never see."

Miss Evans blushed and bobbed a curtsey, and Ivy reflected the young lady was a bit more robust and brightly colored than Ophelia should be. Still, this was as good as a trip to the theater. She had not had so much to entertain her in a year.

"And this," continued Ravensby, "is Mr. Frederick Finestone, who may be depended upon to step into any role at a moment's notice. He is infinitely versatile. He has played the nurse in *Romeo and Juliet*, and in *The Rivals* he was magnificent as—"

"And he was spectacular as a singing tree in the pantomime last Christmas," inserted a stout little fellow, chuckling.

Mr. Finestone looked pained by this contribution, Mr. Ravensby annoyed at the interruption, and the rest of the company amused.

"Miss Durrell, you must be careful of your complexion! The fire is much too hot for you," exclaimed Rosa Evans suddenly.

Sterling had pulled a chair quite close to the fire for her, and at this remark he hurried to move a fireplace screen to protect her from its heat. Miss Durrell smiled at him graciously.

Just at this moment, Wheeling, summoned by the desperate Gerald and looking quite overcome by the unaccustomed duties laid upon him, appeared to conduct the newcomers to their chambers. Gerald, two maids, and a second footman hurried in his wake.

"We will dine at seven, Miss Durrell," Alistair Sterling murmured, taking her hand as she rose from her chair, "and I shall look forward to seeing you again."

Her smile was warm, and Ivy, still watching from above, could feel its magnetism even at this distance. For a brief moment, she felt almost sorry for her uncle, who was receiving its full force. She watched as the others filed up the stairs behind Wheeling, following him obediently to their chambers, most of them glancing around in awe at the impressive Hall.

Silently, she and MacTavish made their way down

to Sterling, who still stared into the flames, mesmerized by the beauty he had just seen.

"Uncle," she ventured, coming close to him without being noticed. "Uncle, can you hear me?"

He looked up abruptly. "Gwen?" he said blankly, almost as if he did not recognize her.

She stared at him a moment. "No, Uncle. It's Ivy. Don't you recognize me?"

"Yes, yes, of course I do," he murmured, straightening his shoulders and for the first time looking her in the eye. "What do you wish, Ivy?"

"You said dinner would be at seven. I was just wondering, Uncle, if you had thought about what you will be able to offer them," she ventured. "I daresay Cook was not prepared for a dozen more people, and she hasn't a great deal of time to fix a meal."

Sterling's eyes widened. "No, I hadn't considered it at all, but I'm certain she will be able to manage." He looked at Ivy hesitantly. "Don't you think so?"

Ivy nodded. "Although I daresay she might wish to speak with someone about it. I was thinking that serving supper fare instead of a formal dinner might be wise—particularly since we have such a large group."

Sterling looked at her a moment. "Yes, I suppose that could be a problem. I must confess that, since I do not entertain, this is something I've given no thought to," he replied slowly. "Can you take care of that kind of thing? Talking with the cook and arranging the supper?"

Ivy nodded. "Of course I can, Uncle. I watched Mama do it regularly."

"Well then, by all means do so," he said decisively. "Miss Durrell must have a respectable meal. As must the others, of course," he added hastily.

"MacTavish and I will see to it immediately," she assured him. Leaving him musing in front of the fire, the two of them set out briskly for the kitchen, the terrier particularly interested in their undertaking.

"What do you think, Mac?" she inquired lightly. "Do you think Mr. Montgomery would enjoy scalloped oysters and mayonnaise of fowl? And a hot soup to ward off the cold?"

A throaty growl from her companion assured her she was thinking along the right lines. All in all, she thought, smoothing her gown, this was turning out to be a much better day than she had thought possible. Her uncle could not very well forbid her to attend a supper she had arranged.

Plunging into the sacred precincts of the kitchen, a room she had visited several times since Miss Willowby's departure, she discovered Mrs. McGrundy, the cook, almost as overwhelmed as Wheeling by the onslaught of so many strangers.

"Well, what's to do, miss?" she asked, her cheeks scarlet as she chopped leeks desperately. "I was fixing a lovely salmon in shrimp sauce with some nice braised leeks for you and your uncle, but I'd no notion it would have to serve fourteen instead of two. And what we are to do with them if this storm continues don't bear thinking about! Why—"

"It's all right, Mrs. McGrundy," Ivy said soothingly. "Everyone knows you've been greatly imposed on, and we all sympathize with you. Whatever you can prepare for supper we will find delightful."

Mrs. McGrundy sniffed disbelievingly. "Those are pretty words, miss, but your uncle is that particular about his food. He says he isn't, of course, that anything is all right with him—and so it is, until he don't like it."

"I'm certain he will appreciate your efforts. Why, just think how good your venison pasties are. He's never complained of those, has he?"

"Well, no, miss, but—"

"I should think he has not! No one could do anything but love them. And you could prepare those, couldn't you?"

"Of course I could, miss, but—"

"And do you have anything put aside for my uncle's dinner tomorrow?" she asked, deftly cutting off the next protest.

She nodded grudgingly. "James had just brought in some lobsters ordered special from London. You know how fond your uncle is of those."

Ivy had no idea how fond her uncle was of anything, but she nodded. "Well, there you are then! Fix those lobsters for tonight."

The cook's eyes widened and her red cheeks grew even redder. "But, miss, we don't have enough for such a group as this!"

"Not to serve buttered lobster, perhaps," Ivy countered, "but you could fix a very nice lobster salad. And those leeks would make a lovely hot soup that would help our guests to thaw a little bit. And perhaps some mushroom fritters?"

Mrs. McGrundy nodded, and together they painstakingly worked out the details, including having Betty, one of the kitchen maids, make fresh raisin cakes to be served with coffee after the supper.

Well pleased with her efforts, Ivy emerged from the kitchen to go in search of Wheeling to arrange the wine for supper, as well as the brandy and port for the gentlemen. During her years with her parents, it had been her observation that an evening ran smoothly if the host supplied a generous amount of inviting food and drink.

This, she thought, smiling to herself and thinking of Mr. Edmund Montgomery, promised to be a most interesting evening.

Four

Within two hours, Mrs. McGrundy, inspired to new culinary heights by the demands placed upon her, had assembled a supper appetizing enough to please any London gentleman.

"For I understand one of them is just that," she commented to Ivy, growing a little more sociable as she finished the last of the fritters and readjusted her cap firmly. "Wheeling says the first one to arrive, Mr. Westbrook, has a gentleman's bearing and a gentleman's tailor, for all he don't have a valet with him. Gerald is drying and polishing his boots for him, and he says he's not seen leather that fine, even the master's boots."

"Yes, I daresay," agreed Ivy, not at all interested in Westbrook. "What does Wheeling say of the others?" Miss Willowby would have been horrified to know she was gossiping with the servants, but, for the moment at least, she didn't care about that. She was eager to hear more about the Montgomerys.

Mrs. McGrundy sniffed and her dark eyebrows rose to the edge of her cap. "Them!" she exclaimed, her tone that of one who has just discovered a mouse drowned in the creampot. "I never thought I'd see the day I'd be laying down my head under the same roof with *playactors!* I told Wheeling to count the silver twice over tonight and to be good and certain he's locked it up tight before he goes to bed."

Ivy did not allow herself to smile at this. "Oh, I don't think it's as bad as all that, Mrs. McGrundy. After all, they were on their way to the Earl of Lakeside, and he certainly wouldn't hire a band of thieves."

Mrs. McGrundy nodded knowingly. "That's what they *say,*" she said ominously. "But how are we to know it's the truth? Perhaps it's just a trick to get them inside the hall so they can steal us blind and murder us all in our beds."

"But they couldn't have conjured up the storm," Ivy protested. "Surely you agree with that, Mrs. McGrundy."

But Mrs. McGrundy was not to be convinced. "I know what I know," she said irrefutably. "And when I go to bed tonight, I'm barring my door—and you'd best do the same, miss."

"I will indeed," Ivy said reassuringly, anxious to turn the conversation to their other guests. "But certainly since we have several manservants, as well as my uncle and Mr. Westbrook and the other two gentlemen, we will be quite safe."

Before Mrs. McGrundy could disabuse her of any such notion, Ivy hurried on. "All of the gentlemen appear quite strong—particularly the two brothers who arrived just after Mr. Westbrook."

The cook shrugged. "I'm sure I couldn't say about that, miss, not having seen them."

Ivy tried again. "Well, what does Wheeling say of them? Are they gentlemen like Mr. Westbrook?"

Mrs. McGrundy shook her head. "Not like him. Mr. Westbrook is quality, born and bred, but Wheeling says the two young gentlemen seem respectable enough. One of them has some books and a Bible in his traveling gear."

Mrs. McGrundy obviously considered this a strong claim to respectability, and Ivy did not take issue with her. Convinced she had learned all she probably could without setting the cook off on another tirade about the actors, Ivy again praised her efforts toward supper and turned toward the door. MacTavish, who had been enjoying a tidbit of venison in front of the kitchen hearth, joined her reluctantly, looking back wistfully at Betty, who had supplied the treat.

Having made certain a fire had been lighted in the yellow saloon, where coffee would be served after supper, Ivy made her way back to the Great Hall. Most of the guests, she was certain, would appear there reasonably soon. For all its vast draftiness, the fire on the huge hearth made it seem welcoming, and the Aubusson carpet lent warmth to the stone floor.

"Ah, Miss Sterling! I knew it was you long before you appeared," said Mr. Westbrook, who was standing with his back to the fire.

"Indeed, sir," she returned, displeased he should be the first to arrive. "And do I walk so heavily, then?"

Westbrook glanced down at MacTavish, who was

returning his gaze. "I believe the telltale walk belongs to someone else," he responded. "I could hear the little beast's toenails clicking against first the wood and then the stone. It's a good thing your uncle does not keep a pack of spaniels in the house. He would never be able to hear himself think unless he kept them on the carpets."

"My uncle does not care for dogs," responded Ivy absently, watching the stairs.

"I must confess he does have a point," said Westbrook, still eying MacTavish.

Just then Edmund Montgomery and his brother appeared at the top of the stairs, and Ivy smiled, her cheeks growing pink. Westbrook glanced up at the two young men, then back at Ivy, his eyebrows lifting slightly.

"Is there no other lady of the house present, ma'am?" he inquired. "Your aunt or your mother?"

"No," she returned briefly, her eyes following Edmund Montgomery. "My uncle has never married, and my own mother is dead."

"A governess, then?"

Stung by his implication, Ivy glared at him. "And why would you be interested in whether or not I have a governess, sir?"

"It occurred to me a young lady like yourself, particularly one who has not yet come out, should not be unchaperoned in a company such as this," he replied.

"I am very nearly eighteen and have no need of a governess!" she told him indignantly, her dark eyes sparkling with anger. "Indeed, sir, I am the one who has superintended the preparation of your supper tonight, so I believe I am fully capable of eating it in company without having someone to look after me!"

"Forgive me, ma'am, for interfering in your private affairs," he said, according her a brief bow. "I did not intend to offend you."

"I daresay you meant to do just that!" she retorted, her eyes having returned to Edmund Montgomery. "You seem not to care about anyone's feelings but your own."

Westbrook appeared to consider her words for a moment, then nodded. "I believe that is an accurate statement, ma'am. It has never been quite clear to me just *why* I should concern myself about the feelings of others—particularly when I don't know what they are."

That won him a brief, disbelieving glance. "I can see you mean it," she observed. "What a very selfish man you must be!"

"Once again, ma'am, you are correct—but again I cannot see why I should be otherwise. Of whom should I be thinking, if not myself?"

"Why, of your family!" she exclaimed. "Or of your friends—assuming, of course, you do have some."

"I have no family," he responded. "And although I do, despite your doubts, have at least one or two friends, they do not expect me to be always thinking of them. In fact, I think they would be quite horrified if I were to do so—and so who does that leave me to think of save myself?"

Ignoring him, she moved toward the Montgomerys and curtseyed briefly as the gentlemen bowed. Miss Durrell and her troupe came eddying down the stairs behind them. Edmund Montgomery gave Ivy his arm and led her back to the fire, although at some distance from Westbrook.

"How charming you look, Miss Sterling," he said, his eyes bringing her as much warmth as the fire. "I must confess I have been looking forward to this moment for some two hours."

"We are of a like mind there, sir," said the literal-minded young man, appearing abruptly beside them. "I am fair famished myself. I've et nothing since a currant bun and a mug of ale this morning."

Ivy and Montgomery stared at him in amazement, and not simply because of his words. The young man, apparently in honor of the occasion, had put on a neckcloth that rose so far above his neck that getting his fork safely past it to his mouth would be no small accomplishment. And although his cherry-striped waistcoat appeared sharply at odds with his orange jacket, the young man— whose name, he informed them, was Jarvis, Melvin Jarvis—held himself proudly, obviously feeling he was arrayed in his best and blended nicely with the crowd.

And, glancing at his companions, Ivy was forced to concede this was true. A peacock, she thought, could have done no better at displaying every color imaginable. The Montgomerys and Westbrook were simply dressed in dark jackets and her uncle had not yet appeared, but the other gen-

tlemen present, and the ladies, appeared to have
rifled the troupe's costume trunk for their finery.
The lantern-jawed little man, a Mr. Sneed, was attired in a jacket, breeches, and lace of the previous
century.

"All he lacks is a wig and patches," murmured
Edmund Montgomery.

"I thought patches were for the ladies," Ivy responded with a low laugh.

At that moment Wheeling and her uncle appeared, and as the elderly butler announced that
dinner was served, Alistair Sterling offered Miss
Durrell his arm.

"And, Miss Sterling, because I am the first wayfarer brought in by the storm, may I claim the
honor of being your escort?" asked Mr. Westbrook
briskly, bowing and offering her his arm.

Thoroughly irritated, Ivy was forced to smile and
accept, for to do otherwise would have been ill
mannered. Because of the motley array of guests,
Ivy had not thought about the order of going in to
dinner. She gave Mr. Montgomery a smile and a
brief curtsey and walked with Mr. Westbrook in her
uncle's wake. MacTavish followed briskly, prepared
to take his place beside his mistress's chair.

"Don't pout, Miss Sterling. It is not becoming,"
Westbrook admonished her.

"I'm not pouting!" she retorted. "You take too
much upon yourself, sir!"

"Naturally I do," he agreed.

"Well, you should not!" she replied sharply. "I did
not wish you to be my escort!"

"Yes, but that does not matter at all, since I wished it," he responded affably.

Ivy fairly shook vexation. "You are an impossible man!"

"I believe we had settled that earlier, Miss Sterling," he reminded her gently. "I do hope you are not inclined to be repetitive, ma'am. I had hoped for rather more in a dinner partner."

"Perhaps another time you will be quick enough to offer for Miss Durrell," she said waspishly, glancing to the end of the table, where her uncle was seating the actress on his right. The candlelight glowed on her rich chestnut hair so it seemed to take on a life of its own, and Alistair Sterling appeared to be aware of no one else in the room.

Mr. Westbrook followed her glance. "Perhaps I shall," he said thoughtfully. "Your uncle is to be envied."

Ivy ignored him as she took her place at the other end of the table, and he seated himself upon her left. To her horror, Mr. Jarvis claimed the place on her right, congratulating himself for doing so.

"I trust conversation with me is looking more appealing, ma'am," Westbrook said in a low voice, as the others noisily arranged themselves. The group of actors had been a little intimidated by their surroundings and the procession in to dinner, but the sight of food seemed to revive them.

"Please," said Ivy, managing to lift her voice above the confusion, "we have not attempted to achieve a formal dinner with all its courses, but instead have prepared a supper we hope you will find enjoyable."

The assembled company appeared to think well of her idea, and the theatrical portion of it seemed strongly inclined to applaud it, but Mr. Ravensby managed to bring them to order.

Ivy nodded to Wheeling, who in turn nodded to the two footmen, and together they handed round Mrs. McGrundy's leek soup, followed closely by lobster salad and the mushroom fritters. Gerald began filling the wine glasses, an action accompanied by sounds of deep appreciation, again from the theatrical company.

"I salute you, Miss Sterling," said Mr. Westbrook, glancing down the table at the group of happy guests, obviously satisfied with their meal. "You have done a notable job of commanding your household to meet this emergency."

"Thank you, sir," she replied bleakly, her gaze upon Edmund Montgomery and Miss Rosa Evans, his dinner partner. He leaned close to the actress, apparently to hear her better, and their conversation appeared merry.

"Don't grind your teeth, Miss Sterling! It is considered very bad form," he reproved her. "Instead, you might behave as though you find my company captivating. You would not wish to appear too eager."

Ivy flushed. "But I do not find your company captivating, Mr. Westbrook, and I am no actress!"

"My point precisely, ma'am! You must learn to be one. If you wander about with your heart on your sleeve for all to see, you may be certain your experience will very often be a painful one."

"And is that from your own experience, sir?" she asked, moving to the attack. "Did you at one time wear your heart on your sleeve?"

"Never," he assured her. "But I am a great observer of the human condition, and I know that to be true."

Fortunately, at that moment Mr. Jarvis solicited her attention so he might propose her health, which was warmly drunk by all the company, and that of her uncle, to which they once again drank.

The dinner finally wound down, despite Mr. Jarvis's attempt to drink the health of all those present and of many who were absent. Ivy carried on a desultory conversation with Mr. Westbrook, but she waited eagerly for the moment when she could stand, signaling the ladies' exit to the yellow saloon, where the gentlemen would join them after brandy and cigars.

Ivy, Miss Durrell, Miss Evans, and two other ladies made their way to the drawing room, MacTavish following them closely. Having been denied any opportunity of conversing with Mr. Edmund Montgomery thus far, Ivy was determined to make up for it during the evening. She had caught his eye several times during dinner, and she was certain he was equally interested, so she hoped the gentlemen did not linger.

Five

One thing Ivy had not considered was what she would discuss with the ladies while they were waiting for the gentlemen to appear. As they gathered in the yellow saloon, she smiled at the others, and said pleasantly, "We do have a pianoforte, but I fear that I have no gift for music. Perhaps one of you would like to play?"

The others glanced at one another, and Miss Evans moved quickly to it. She began a number that sounded like something that would be heard just before a comedy piece at the theater, and Miss Durrell caught the young lady's eye. Immediately the music changed, becoming more sedate.

"Well, Miss Sterling, I must compliment you," said Miss Durrell in her inimitable voice. It was a husky, intimate voice, Ivy thought, thick like the golden honey she spread on her toast.

"Compliment me, ma'am?" she asked, her brows lifted. "I thank you, of course, but I can't think why you would be complimenting me."

"I understand from your uncle you are the one who marshaled the servants to prepare such a comfortable supper for us all," Miss Durrell replied, leaning closer to her. "That was quite a task, my dear, and you handled it superbly."

Ivy felt herself glowing from the compliment, and she began to understand a little of Miss Durrell's power. She made her listeners feel as though they were the only ones in the world of importance while she was speaking to them. Aside from a lovely face and an unforgettable voice, Miss Durrell had the enviable capacity to concentrate her attention upon the person at hand. When one was that person, everyone and everything else became unimportant.

"You're very kind, ma'am," Ivy returned, flushing despite herself. "I quite enjoyed it, however."

"I can well imagine that," returned the actress. "I could see at a glance you are not just another pretty face. You have insight and initiative, and no one can teach you those. Those gifts, combined with your face and fortune, will take you wherever you wish to go, my dear."

"Thank you, Miss Durrell," Ivy murmured, feeling as though she had received a benediction.

The other two ladies seemed engaged in conversation of their own. Or, more accurately, one of them, a rather plain, birdlike woman of indeterminate age, chattered in a low voice at the other. The chatterer, Ivy remembered, was a Miss Floyd, and her victim was a Mrs. Rollins, a voluptuous woman unmistakably wearing rouge and, Ivy suspected, something on her brows and eyelids as well. Miss Durrell's makeup, on the other hand, was gracefully discreet, lacking Mrs. Rollins's vermilion cheeks.

"You must often be lonely here," commented Miss Durrell, her eyes fixed on Ivy's, "without any other feminine society."

"Oh, indeed I am," sighed Ivy, glad to have someone interested in her predicament. "I have wished very much to go to London and have my coming out, but my uncle has not wished me to go."

Miss Durrell's tawny eyes glinted in the candlelight. "Well, we shall have to see what we can do about that, my dear," she said lightly. "Of course you wish for the society of other young people. It is only natural."

"Oh, thank you," said Ivy gratefully. "I would be so grateful if you could convince him." And if anyone could, she thought earnestly, it would be this very lady, under whose spell her uncle appeared to have fallen.

"It would be a very good thing for your uncle as well," Miss Durrell observed. "I believe he has spent very little time in society himself."

"You are correct, of course," agreed Ivy, losing a little of her enthusiasm. She really did not care whether her uncle enjoyed society or not, so long as he allowed her to go to London. "When he leaves Foxridge Hall, he goes only to other isolated places in Scotland or the north so he may hunt and fish."

The actress shrugged gracefully. "Then it is more than time he had a change of pace, I think." She glanced at Ivy. "And that would naturally mean a change of pace for you as well."

"That would be wonderful," Ivy nodded, "but I fear that—"

Before she could explain to Miss Durrell that her uncle was a most difficult man, Wheeling opened the door and the gentlemen entered the saloon, Alistair Sterling leading the way.

Surprised they had been so brief a time over their brandy and cigars, particularly given Mr. Jarvis's propensity to propose toasts, Ivy watched her uncle bear down upon them, his eyes fixed upon Miss Durrell.

"I hope you are quite comfortable, ma'am," he murmured to her. "Do you find the room a little chilly?"

"No indeed, sir," she responded, her smile unfolding like a flower. Ivy had never seen a smile begin so lazily at the corners of the lips and grow so perceptibly to be a warm, full-lipped smile. Neither, apparently, had her uncle, she thought as she glanced at him.

Miss Durrell patted Ivy on the arm. "I was just complimenting your niece, sir, on how well she has provided for our comfort."

Alistair Sterling spared Ivy a brief glance of approval, but reverted immediately to his guest. Ivy, taking the hint, rose hastily so he could take her place on the sofa.

As she rose, Edmund Montgomery hurried to her side. "Please, Miss Sterling," he murmured, "won't you take a brief walk around the room with me? I feel the need of at least a little exercise, and I daresay you feel the same."

Happily, she accepted his arm. It was, she thought, an admirable plan, for it would keep Mr.

Jarvis and Mr. Westbrook at bay—at least for a little while.

"Tell me, Miss Sterling, did you not find the number of toasts at supper excessive?" he asked in a low voice, his expression amused.

"I must confess I thought I would be compelled to do him damage were there another," she responded lightly, laughing.

"Then you must feel for me, ma'am, abandoned as I was to his tender mercies when you and the other ladies left. I assure you he began it all again."

"I have no doubt of it," she assured him, "and my heart ached for you and the other gentlemen stranded there." She paused a moment. "In truth, I was surprised to see you appear so quickly. I had quite made up my mind you would be at least an hour."

"Not a bit of it," he said staunchly. "I was determined to make my way to your side as soon as possible. Every moment spent there was time I might be spending with you."

"How kind you are," she murmured, not meeting his eyes for a moment. This was, of course, precisely what she wished to hear, but it had taken her a little by surprise.

To her annoyance, Wheeling opened the door just then and two maids bore in the trays for coffee. Curtseying to Mr. Montgomery, she went to superintend the affair, closely attended by MacTavish, who was fond of cakes.

The appearance of food and drink once again produced a convivial rustling among the others.

Miss Floyd, tasting one of the raisin cakes, fluttered enthusiastically, urging everyone to try them. Indeed, Ivy could see at a glance she would have to ring for Wheeling—and she hoped that Betty had made as many of the cakes as Ivy had recommended.

By the time she had made her arrangements and returned her attention to Mr. Montgomery, she saw Miss Evans had left the pianoforte and was attempting to feed him a bite of a raisin cake, which he was laughingly refusing. Finally, he gave in and accepted it. Ivy noticed with irritation that the actress's fingers lingered on his lips.

"It is a pity you had coffee served in here rather than in the Great Hall, Miss Sterling," observed Mr. Westbrook, following her gaze.

"Why do you say so, sir?" she inquired, interested not at all in his answer.

"Why, because that is where all the weaponry is displayed on the walls, of course."

Startled, she looked up at him.

"Well, that is what you were wishing for, is it not, ma'am? A sword? Or perhaps merely one of those wicked looking daggers?" He glanced at Mr. Montgomery and Miss Evans and then leaned toward her, lowering his voice. "Remember what I told you, ma'am. Do not wear your heart on your sleeve for all to see."

Humiliated at being caught out once again and fearful of being obvious, she satisfied her need for vengeance by snapping at him. "One would think, Mr. Westbrook, that you would have something better to do than to observe my actions and belittle me!"

He nodded. "One would think so, to be sure," he agreed, adding, "Don't curl your lip, ma'am. It is not at all becoming. You must learn to school your countenance so you do not give away each emotion."

Before she could retort, he continued blandly, "However, if you but look about you, you will see I am quite limited in subjects for observation. Your uncle is with the only other woman of interest in the room, and I have had quite enough of the company of the gentlemen during our brief but delightful interlude over brandy."

"I am delighted you enjoyed your time with them," she replied, her tone acidic, but her expression pleasant.

"Oh, much better, Miss Sterling," he said approvingly. "You deliver—or attempt to deliver—a verbal dagger while smiling at the blood you expect to draw. With a few more lessons, you will be adequately prepared for your coming out."

Ivy thought for a moment, and he watched her appreciatively, certain she was struggling for an appropriate retort.

Smiling beatifically at Westbrook, she put out her hand to stop Mr. Jarvis, who was just passing them.

"Mr. Jarvis," she said, smiling up at that weedy young man, "Mr. Westbrook and I were just discussing how admirably you phrased the healths you proposed at supper."

"Indeed?" he said, his gaunt face glowing. Praise was a rare commodity for Mr. Jarvis.

"Yes, we certainly were," she assured him. "Pray excuse me a moment, for I must see to Miss Floyd, who is alone on the sofa. However, I know Mr. Westbrook would be most grateful if you could share with him a few of your favorite toasts, for, as I said, he was greatly struck by your use of language this evening."

Ivy smiled again at her victim, who was glaring at her, then turned and made her way lightly to Miss Floyd.

"And how do you find yourself, Miss Floyd?" she asked, sitting down beside that lady. "Would you perhaps like to sit closer to the fire? You are shivering a little."

Miss Floyd looked at her gratefully, drawing a thin shawl about her bony shoulders. "Yes, Miss Sterling, that would be lovely indeed, but I don't want to be an inconvenience to anyone."

"Nonsense," Ivy reassured her, drawing a chair close to the fire and supplying that lady with a firescreen to protect her from its full heat. She had just instructed one of the maids to take Miss Floyd another cup of coffee and a cake when she observed Reginald Ravensby bearing down upon her.

"Miss Sterling," he said, his voice making her name sound like a trumpet call, "may I thank you for your gracious hospitality, ma'am?" He bent over her hand, and for a moment she feared he was about to kiss it, so she snatched it to safety.

"You are very kind, sir," she replied absently, trying to see if Mr. Montgomery still attended Miss Evans.

"Do sit down, dear lady," said Ravensby, guiding her to the sofa recently vacated by Miss Floyd. "I have come to try to repay our debt by telling you some of the stories you are so eager to hear."

"Stories?" she asked, startled. For the first time she gave him her full attention. "What stories, sir?"

"Why, stories about my theatrical career, of course," he said, settling himself upon the sofa. "I would have had no notion you were so interested in hearing about it had Mr. Westbrook not informed me of it. He told me you were shy of asking me yourself, not wishing to appear forward, but I assure you I will be delighted to tell you."

Her eyes flew to meet Westbrook's. He was still engaged in conversation with Mr. Jarvis, but his eyes met hers, his eyebrows rose, and a brief smile creased his face.

"It all began when I was no more than a lad," Ravensby began, and Ivy resigned herself to her evening, trying to keep her countenance from betraying her once again.

Briefly she wondered if she should call Wheeling and have him open the windows in Westbrook's chamber so that it would be properly aired for the evening, with a drift of snow left upon his counterpane. That thought sustained her while she gazed at the storyteller, who was beginning chapter one of the first volume of his career.

Six

Ivy awoke early the next morning, sharply conscious that she had duties. Even if she had been inclined to forget them, MacTavish was busily reminding her, growling softly at her now and then to suggest dogs also had their needs. After lying still for a moment, she remembered the events of the previous day and smiled. For a moment she wondered whether or not she had actually had Wheeling open Mr. Westbrook's windows, but decided she had not had the opportunity to do so. At any rate, she intended for breakfast to be properly laid out in the dining room, and she was equally determined that this morning she would spend some time with Mr. Edmund Montgomery before he and his brother had to depart, regardless of Mr. Westbrook.

The chambermaid had already been in, so her fire was crackling happily, and MacTavish had left his basket to lie in front of it. Ivy hurried to wash, select a becoming dress of Irish green kerseymere, and bind her dark curls in matching ribbons. Before leaving her chamber, she hurried over to open her drapes. What she saw caused her to stand perfectly still. The snow was still coming down. Indeed, the wind had driven some onto the windowsill inside her chamber. Insofar as she could see, the world outside was perfectly white.

Mrs. McGrundy had been correct, she thought ruefully. She had not thought they would really have to worry about guests for more than one night, but the cook had been wise to consider the possibility. As she hurried down the stairs, her terrier at her heels, she tried to think through what their supplies were. She had taken a brief look through the larder and the pantry as they were planning last night's supper. If the roads were impassable, as they surely would be, they might well be so tomorrow, for the snow was still falling thickly. How many days could they accommodate so large a party? she wondered.

When Ivy arrived in the kitchen, she quickly discovered Mrs. McGrundy had been making the same calculations.

"I think, miss, that unless this storm lasts for a fortnight, we will be able to take care of all of us, family and guests and servants alike. Thank heaven I sent Betty to the game larder before the storm. We will not be starving."

"You relieve my mind, Mrs. McGrundy, for I admit I had not thought about the storm lasting. I have never seen a snowstorm last so long before."

"I remember one from my girlhood, miss, which is why I began thinking about what we had available to us," responded the cook, earnestly kneading the dough that would shortly become breakfast rolls.

"My sister and I were staying at our mother's cottage to care for her, and we did not have enough set by to see us through such a long and miserable storm. The wood ran out, too."

Ivy stared at her. "The food and wood both ran out? Why, Mrs. McGrundy, whatever did you do?"

The cook shrugged. "We chopped up the wooden chest that held my bridal linens, along with our table and a bench—all our furniture except Mother's bed—and we set a snare for rabbits not too far outside our front door."

"You chopped up all your furniture?" Ivy asked, feeling as though she could do little other than repeat Mrs. McGrundy's words. "But how terrible for you, Mrs. McGrundy."

"We were luckier than some," she responded briskly, shaping the dough into rolls. "There were some that did not live through that time. Our neighbors froze in their cottage."

Ivy's eyes widened at this flat statement. "They died?" she asked.

Mrs. McGrundy nodded. "Froze, they did. My sister and I went over as soon as we could get out of our cottage, for we knew they were an old couple and might have trouble." A tear rolled down her cheek and she absently wiped it away with the back of one floury hand. "We found them in front of the fire, although it had burnt out long ago. They were sitting there next to each other on the settle, with a laprobe over them."

"How terrible," said Ivy, touched by this long-ago tragedy and sinking down on their own settle in front of a fire that showed no signs of going out.

"Yes, it was," Mrs. McGrundy agreed. "It were many a long night before I could rest easy in my sleep. I would look out my window at their little cottage away at the bottom of the hill and think about them and their fifty years of marriage."

"Fifty years!" exclaimed Ivy, and Betty, who was also laboring over dough, looked equally impressed.

"They were a rare old couple," remarked the cook, placing a tray of rolls in the oven next to the fire. "I think about them now and then and tell Sam we are that fortunate to have a certain home here with Mr. Sterling."

"And your husband oversees the stables, does he not?" Ivy inquired, a little ashamed that she really did not know, although she had lived at the Hall for a year.

Again Mrs. McGrundy nodded agreeably. "Sam has been in Mr. Sterling's service these twenty years and more, and I have been here almost as long."

Ivy, curious to ask if her uncle were a good employer, was about to inquire when MacTavish, standing by the kitchen door, gave one imperative bark.

"Excuse me, Mrs. McGrundy. MacTavish hasn't been out yet this morning," she said, hurrying to the door.

"You're never going to let the little tyke out in this terrible weather!" exclaimed the cook. "Why, he'll get lost before you can turn around good."

As she opened the door, Ivy was inclined to agree

with her, but the little dog gave her one reproach-
ful look, as though she had indeed conjured up this
terrible weather, and plowed into the drift that had
blown against the door. Ivy watched anxiously, fearful she had made a mistake, but MacTavish
reappeared in a matter of seconds, well coated with
snow but looking very satisfied.

"Good dog!" she exclaimed, catching him up in
the towel she had brought down from her chamber
for this express purpose. Drying him expertly, she
released him in front of the fire to roll happily on
the braided mat.

"I am afraid he didn't go very far away from the
door to take care of matters," Ivy said delicately to
Mrs. McGrundy. "I trust no one will step into his
mess and track it in."

"I wouldn't imagine so, miss," the cook responded, preparing a second tray of rolls for the
oven. "We've little enough traffic in and out
today."

A comfortable silence ensued while Mrs. Mc-
Grundy sliced ham and Ivy made a more careful
inspection of the larder and the pantry, planning
possible menus for the next three days. She had
just returned to the warmth of the kitchen and
freshly baked rolls when the back door swung open
and an icy blast of air once more swept through the
room. Even MacTavish and Mrs. McGrundy's calico
cat, now dozing peacefully in front of the fire, were
disturbed by the cold and turned to determine its
cause.

A figure coated in snow slammed the door behind him and exclaimed loudly, "Do you have anything hot to drink, Mrs. McGrundy? I am fairly frozen to the bone by this ungodly weather!"

"Indeed I do, sir," she exclaimed cheerfully, bustling about to prepare a mug of hot cider. "Sit down here on the settle, sir, and warm yourself before you go any farther. It's far too cold to be out on a morning such as this!"

"I had to see to my horse," he explained. "And I've taken the liberty of hooking a rope from the kitchen door across to the stable door. I trust no one will mind."

Betty glanced up from her baking in surprise. "A rope? Why would you need a rope, sir?" she asked, and then blushed because her curiosity had betrayed her into speaking to her betters.

"So I can get safely there and back," he replied. "The snow is so thick out there you could get lost in the blink of an eyelash and wander about until you froze in a snowbank."

Betty shuddered, but Ivy returned briskly, "Well, we certainly would not wish to lose you to a snowbank, Mr. Westbrook."

He glanced up in surprise. "Miss Sterling! Forgive me, I did not see you there. I daresay it's because of the snow still clinging to my lashes and brows so that I'm half blind."

He chuckled, taking a sip from his mug of steaming cider. "Of course, I suppose it's for the best you didn't know I was out there."

"Why do you say so, sir?" she asked curiously.

"I daresay I would have been worried about your

chopping off my guide rope from this end if you had known where I was."

Ivy flushed. "You mustn't be saying things you don't mean, Mr. Westbrook. Mrs. McGrundy won't know that you are only joking."

Westbrook had picked up the towel she had used on MacTavish and left drying over a screen near the hearth and was proceeding to dry his face upon it.

"But I'm not, as you very well know, ma'am. I count myself lucky to be sitting here in safety with you instead of wandering through the storm."

Mrs. McGrundy laughed. "Don't mind him, miss. He likes a joke, as you can see." She glanced up from her work to see him still busily drying his face and hair and gasped. "Oh, sir! Do let me get you a clean towel!"

"What's wrong with this one?" he asked, looking down at it. As he did so, he saw dark curly hairs on the towel that he hadn't noticed before, and he heard Ivy laughing.

"I believe that some of these are a bit too short and curly to be mine," he observed grimly, plucking one. He glanced down at MacTavish, warmly ensconced on the rug, and the little dog, feeling his gaze, stared up at Westbrook with liquid eyes.

"Yes, I might have known," he said to the dog. "I suppose you were out taking care of affairs of your own. At least I didn't—" he began, then paused and inspected the soles of his boots closely. The first inspection revealed nothing, but the second yielded an unpleasant surprise.

"If it were possible, you little beast," said Westbrook ominously, "I would swear you did that deliberately."

"There now, sir, don't fret over it!" exclaimed the cook. "Just you sit down here, and I'll call one of the footmen to take care of that for you."

Ivy bent over her pet and stroked his head. "There, there, Mac," she said soothingly. "Don't take it to heart. You're a good boy."

"That's right," said Westbrook bitterly. "Every time the little beast serves me a backhand turn, there you are to congratulate him and urge him on to new heights. I fear to think what could be next."

Ivy laughed heartily, beginning to feel this was more satisfying than having the windows left open in his chamber. Far better, she thought, to enjoy his discomfort in person. She sat down next to him on the settle and regarded him curiously. "Tell me again, Mr. Westbrook, just why you were plunging about out there in the storm."

"To take care of my horse," he responded.

"But couldn't the stablehands take care of him?" she asked. "After all, Mrs. McGrundy's husband Sam is in charge of them. He will see to it your mount is taken care of."

"I'm certain he will," Westbrook responded. "However, my mount is my responsibility, and he knows me, not a stranger."

Ivy shook her head. "That still seems like an extraordinary amount of trouble to take, Mr. Westbrook," she replied. "Nonetheless, I bow to your experience—and I credit you for your interest in the welfare of your horse."

He gave her a brief bow. "I am overcome by your tribute, Miss Sterling. I shall treasure it, I assure you, as the only kind word I am likely ever to receive from you."

"Nonsense!" she retorted. "You refine upon events too much. I have nothing against you, sir."

He looked at her gravely for a moment, the laughter fading from his eyes and voice. "I am glad to hear it, ma'am. I hope that means that you will be willing to listen to a little well-meant advice."

Ivy rose abruptly. "Indeed it does not, Mr. Westbrook. I am in need of none, I do assure you. And," she said, dropping a brief curtsey, "I have much to do to prepare for the other guests, so I pray you will excuse me."

She walked briskly from the kitchen, MacTavish reluctantly parting from the comfort of the fire and the calico cat to follow her.

Seven

Breakfast was a far more casual matter than supper had been, and Ivy was grateful for the difference. The meal was set out on the sideboard in the breakfast parlor, and the guests were free to wander in and eat whenever they arose. The velvet drapes, usually open to allow in the morning sun, were kept tightly drawn today. The wind was rising, and their heaviness helped to keep the room a little warmer. A fire had been burning since early morning to make the room's temperature as bearable as possible, but Ivy noticed everyone wished to sit on the side of the table closer to the fire.

She had posted herself there to be certain the guests were cared for and to suggest what that they might do to while away the day that lay before them. She had hopes the billiard room would be of interest to the gentlemen, and she had secured several old newspapers from her uncle's library, along with a few of her own books and journals, as reading material to be placed in the yellow saloon. She was well aware her uncle regarded his library as sacred territory and none of the guests would be invited there. She had also had Wheeling bring in the chess table and decks of playing cards for the two game tables.

And of course there could, she hoped, be some conversation among the members of the group. The experience of the last evening had not encouraged that hope, but she knew time would hang heavy upon their hands if they did not have something to do. Naturally, she also hoped Mr. Edmund Montgomery would wish to spend some time in conversation with her. She had thought about the prospect most of last night and this morning, imagining what they might say to one another.

She glanced up eagerly each time the door to the breakfast room opened, but almost all of the company had assembled before he put in an appearance. She felt her cheeks warm when he appeared, but Mr. Westbrook, who had entered behind him, caught her eye warningly, so her greeting was a little more constrained than it might otherwise have been.

"Good morning, gentlemen," she murmured. "I hope you slept well."

"Like a top!" exclaimed Edmund Montgomery cheerfully. "I cannot imagine having a better night's sleep!"

Mr. Ravensby, who had been brooding over his sausages for the past half hour, looked at him darkly. "I daresay, sir, you slept well because you are not as sensitive as some of us are."

"Why, I'm sorry, Mr. Ravensby," responded Ivy politely. "Did something interfere with your rest?"

Ravensby tossed his head back and ran one hand gently through his dark, artistically windswept curls—although Ivy noticed he did not muss them at all. "I scarcely laid my head on the pillow, ma'am," he assured her. "So concerned was I for the safety of my little troupe that I paced back and forth in my chamber for most of the night, and from time to time I braved the icy passageway to check upon each of them."

"I say, Reg!" interrupted Mr. Jarvis indignantly. "Was that you rattling at my door in the middle of the night? If it was, you gave me a dashed queer start and unsettled the mushroom fritters I et for supper."

Mr. Ravensby appeared pained by the allusion to the fritters, but he continued manfully. "I could not rest until I knew each of you was safe and warm, for I know only too well what it is to lose a beloved companion."

His voice gathered strength, and Ivy could see he was just beginning. Having had a fair sample of just how long he could go on with a captive audience, she looked about the table desperately, and again caught Mr. Westbrook's eye.

Responding to her unspoken plea, Westbrook abruptly rang the bell for Wheeling. Turning to Mr. Ravensby, he said, "Certainly, sir, as a man whose voice is everything to him, you must do something to ward off the effects of wandering in that icy passageway. I believe I detect a hoarseness in your tone that could take its toll upon your voice unless you rest it."

Ravensby looked startled by this observation, and his hand went involuntarily to his throat. "Do you indeed, sir?" he asked.

Westbrook shook his head decisively. "I would

advise you to drink hot lemon tea and honey as soon as possible, sir, and to do absolutely nothing to agitate your throat."

Ivy nodded, and as Wheeling tottered into the room, she gave him the order for Mrs. McGrundy, and suggested Mr. Ravensby take a place nearer the fire. Gratified by so much attention to his needs, that gentleman allowed himself to be moved to a place of solitary splendor beside the fire, a butler's tray at his elbow for the forthcoming tea and the abandoned sausages.

Breathing a sigh of relief, she turned back to Mr. Montgomery. "I trust you had no such interruptions in your rest, sir," she said, smiling.

"Not a bit of it," he assured her earnestly. "I slept the sleep of the dead."

From the corner of her eye, she could see this allusion to the dead appeared to have caught Mr. Ravensby's attention, but Westbrook put his hand to his own throat as a reminder to the actor and Ravensby nodded, sinking closer to the fire and caressing his own endangered throat.

"I hope this delay in your journey will not be too great an inconvenience to you and your brother, sir," Ivy said, attempting to continue their conversation. She had talked with him so little on the previous evening that she had no notion of who he was nor where he was going.

"No," he said, still smiling at her. "Our commissions will still be waiting, and Randall and I will take ship for North America. We will join our regiment there."

There was a rustle of excitement about the table at this announcement.

"North America!" exclaimed Miss Evans. "How fortunate you are, sir, to be going on such an exciting venture!"

Mr. Montgomery's eyes sparkled. "Indeed, I count myself triply fortunate, Miss Evans. I am to become a lieutenant, I will be serving my country in a faraway place I have always longed to see, and I will be doing so with my brother, who is to serve as chaplain to the regiment!"

"You are indeed a fortunate man," agreed Mr. Westbrook, and most of the others nodded. Ivy, however, took exception to his statement.

"But you are going into a war, sir," she said earnestly. "Should you be in a battle with the Americans, you will be going into great danger!"

Mr. Montgomery nodded enthusiastically. "Indeed, I will be. I have hoped for months for just this opportunity."

Miss Evans placed her hand to her breast and said with great feeling, "But what if something should happen to you, sir? How could your friends—and I count myself as one of them—how could your friends bear such a loss?"

Ivy looked as though she could think of at least one loss she could bear with equanimity, but once again she felt Mr. Westbrook's eyes upon her and she would not give him the satisfaction of a reaction, so she controlled herself admirably.

"And you say your brother will be a chaplain with your regiment?" inquired Ivy coolly.

"Yes, indeed," he responded eagerly. "Randall has given up a very good living in order to do so. He says since I am his only family, he prefers to go with me."

"Then you are extraordinarily fortunate. Not many brothers would do so much for the sake of family," said Ivy, impressed by the absent Mr. Montgomery, who, according to his brother, spent some time alone in reflection and prayer each morning.

"I played a vicar just last year," contributed Mr. Finestone, willing to enter in to the conversation. "Some even said I did it so well they thought I had a vocation for the church." Here he glanced round the table modestly. "Not, of couse, that I'm thinking of becoming a member of the cloth. My heart belongs to the stage."

A stifled sound from Mr. Ravensby reminded them of his presence, and Miss Floyd said in a low voice, "I believe Mr. Ravensby wants us to remember he has played a bishop in two different plays—"

A strangled sound from the direction of the hearth caused her to glance up and add hurriedly, "Forgive me, I believe it must have been *three* different plays, but naturally Mr. Ravensby could not consider leaving the stage for—"

"Yes, yes, we know, Miss Floyd," interrupted Mr. Westbrook. "Being such an ornament of the stage, Mr. Ravensby could not, naturally, sacrifice his art for his religion."

Ravensby, who had been leaning forward with great earnestness, relaxed once again and nodded, as though giving his blessing to Westbrook's words.

Ivy, anxious to divert the conversation to safer

channels and determined to have some time with Mr. Montgomery, said brightly, "Perhaps some of you gentlemen would care to play billiards. My uncle has a well-appointed billiards room."

Mr. Jarvis and Mr. Sneed were eying one another doubtfully, but Mr. Montgomery exclaimed, "Billiards! By all that's wonderful, that will provide us with some entertainment today! What do you say, Westbrook?"

This time Ivy's countenance did betray her, and she felt Westbrook glance at her. Although she wouldn't meet his eyes, she knew by the tone of his answer he was laughing at her.

"I am not a man greatly addicted to the game, Mr. Montgomery, but I daresay I could bear an hour or two of it. Are you certain, however, there is nothing else you would prefer to be doing?"

Montgomery shook his head with great decisiveness. "I have spent many an hour in just this way. Are you a betting man, Westbrook?"

Westbrook looked at the younger man narrowly and shook his head. "I am not so certain of my play as all that, I fear."

Mr. Jarvis and Mr. Sneed, after a hasty, whispered exchange, appeared to feel prepared to undertake the game together, and Mr. Ravensby rose silently from his chair, apparently planning to grace the billiard room with his presence as well.

Ivy forced herself to smile brightly at the rest of the group. "Well, I daresay the rest of us can find something to pass the time in the yellow saloon. If we adjourn there, I know Wheeling has it warm for us."

The mention of warmth appeared to act as a magnet, and the migration to the billiard room and the yellow saloon began immediately. She did not allow herself to register any resentment of Mr. Montgomery's decision to play billiards, however. Certainly it was understandable a young man would wish to have some entertainment with other gentlemen.

"Do you know where my uncle is?" she asked Mr. Westbrook, ignoring his laughing eyes as they moved toward the door. "He has not yet been in for breakfast."

He smiled. "I should imagine he is wherever Miss Durrell is," he replied. "Has it not occurred to you we have seen neither of them this morning?"

Startled, she stared up at him, then turned to Wheeling, who had just entered the room.

"Wheeling, where may I find my uncle?"

"In his library, Miss Sterling. I took in breakfast for him and Miss Durrell."

"I see," she replied, still more surprised. Miss Durrell had been admitted to the inner sanctum. That spoke volumes for how highly her uncle regarded the actress. Interesting though that was, however, she was profoundly annoyed to think that the two of them were enjoying a tête-à-tête while she was saddled with looking after the others.

"Would you like me to beat on the door of the library and demand they come out?" inquired Westbrook innocently. "Or would you prefer to do it yourself?"

"Nonsense!" she snapped. "There is no need to do any such thing!"

He smiled without comment, and Ivy noticed it was difficult to pass the library door without glaring at it.

The next few hours scarcely went as she had expected. The gentlemen, with the exception of her uncle and Mr. Randall Montgomery, retired to the billiard room, while the ladies attempted to make themselves at home in the yellow saloon.

To her horror, Mrs. Rollins suggested a game of whist, and firmly seated the other ladies at one of the card tables.

"Floyd and I always play partners," she announced, "so Miss Sterling, you and Rosa must be partners."

Ivy greatly disliked playing cards and knew herself to be a poor player. "Perhaps we should wait for the gentlemen," she suggested.

Mrs. Rollins laughed abruptly. "If we were to wait for them, we should be very fortunate to have played a single rubber before supper. You are young, Miss Sterling. Do not let your pleasure wait upon the men."

"Now, Dora," fluttered Miss Floyd. "I'm certain if Miss Sterling does not wish to play, we should not force her to do so."

"Of course you are not forcing me," replied Ivy, attempting to be gracious and remember that she was, practically speaking, the hostess. "But I fear I will prove a great disappointment to your game."

"Never mind that," Mrs. Rollins advised her,

shuffling the cards dexterously. "Emily and I enjoy winning, and Rosa is well accustomed to losing."

"Well, I would not be so accustomed, Dora, if you did not insist upon partnering me with someone who has no knowledge of the game."

Sniffing, she sat down opposite to Ivy, and added pettishly, "Someday I will be Emily's partner, Dora, and you will be forced to be on the losing end. Without Emily, you would certainly never win so regularly."

"Oh, I would not say—" began Miss Floyd modestly, but Miss Evans cut her off.

"You know very well you are the real player, Emily. Your partner could be Miss Sterling's little dog, and you would still win."

Mrs. Rollins showed no sign of acknowledging this speech, but Miss Floyd twisted nervously in her chair, aware of her partner's annoyance. As for Ivy, she felt perhaps she should put MacTavish in her place and allow Miss Evans to play their game for them. The next three games passed in a gray fog of misery. The only thing she was perfectly aware of was that she had yet to make one play properly and that Miss Evans had announced and discussed each of her errors. Miss Floyd and MacTavish were the only perfectly happy creatures in the room.

Toward the end of the third game, the door to the saloon opened and Ivy turned toward it desperately. The newcomer was Mr. Randall Montgomery, having finished his morning devotions and his breakfast.

"Why, Mr. Montgomery!" she exclaimed, as

though greeting an old friend. "Do come in and join us! I would be delighted to yield my place to you so you have some way to pass the time, and I will attend to some household matters."

"I am grateful for your kindness," he assured her, "but I was searching for my brother. Can you help me, Miss Sterling?"

"Indeed I can!" she replied, rising from her place. "If you will excuse me, ladies, I must take a moment to help Mr. Montgomery find the billiard room."

"Just ring for the butler, Miss Sterling, and continue your hand," commanded Mrs. Rollins. "We have not yet finished this game."

"The billiard room!" said Mr. Montgomery abruptly. "They are playing billiards?"

"Naturally not," said Mrs. Rollins bitterly as she watched her victim escape. "I daresay they are just standing about the table talking."

"Dora," remonstrated Miss Floyd in a low voice, "Dora, you really must not speak in such a way to our hostess and to a man of the cloth."

"Get the dog," said Miss Evans bitterly. "I could do as well and the game could go on."

In the midst of this bickering, the door opened once more and the gentlemen came flooding in.

The theatrical gentlemen, led by Mr. Jarvis, hurried toward the fire, first holding their hands toward it, then turning and backing toward it. Their flurry of activity disturbed MacTavish, who reluctantly arose and made room for them.

"Do come and play, Jarvis," called Mrs. Rollins

imperiously. "Miss Sterling has been called away from her place and Rosa needs a partner."

"I couldn't hold the cards, Dora. My fingers won't even bend!" he exclaimed, holding up his hand. "I'd swear they've frozen solid!"

"The billiard room was that cold?" asked Ivy anxiously. "Wheeling built a fire."

"It would take ten fires to warm that room," Mr. Sneed assured her, counting his digits as though to be certain none had dropped off along the way. "I daresay there are icicles hanging behind the drapery in there."

"Indeed, I am so very sorry I sent you to such an uncomfortable place," said Ivy, directing her attention to Mr. Edmund Montgomery. "How came you to stay this long when it was so very uncomfortable?"

"The lure of the game, ma'am, the lure of the game," he replied gaily. "When your attention is concentrated on the perfect move, the precise angle of the cue, your body has no time to consider cold."

"Well, mine did!" snapped Sneed. "I think I'm suffering from frostbite right now! And to top if off, I've lost a spade guinea for the honor of freezing to death!"

"I told you laying a wager would not be advisable," observed Mr. Westbrook.

Randall Montgomery looked up sharply at his brother. "You were wagering?" he asked.

"Only in sport," Edmund assured him, "nothing of consequence." He rubbed his hands ruefully. "I must say the others may be right about the cold. I was so caught up in play that I wasn't paying attention to how stiff my hands were becoming. I fear we have done with the billiard room while this weather holds."

Here he looked at Ivy. "I trust you are bored enough, Miss Sterling, to grant me a little of your time. I have been hoping to talk with you about my journey to North America, if you are not too busy with household affairs."

"Oh no, of course not, Mr. Montgomery," she replied happily. "I am not otherwise occupied now."

Miss Evans threw up her hands in disgust, but Ivy was oblivious to everyone else. All she could see was the intent blue gaze of Edmund Montgomery, turned to full effect upon her.

"Perhaps if we walk once again, I can restore some circulation," he said, offering her his arm, and they began their stroll about the room, happily ignoring the others as he told her of his plans.

"After the war is over, we shall sell out and settle there," he said confidently. "Randall and I shall have a new life in a new country."

"You will settle there permanently?" Ivy asked doubtfully. "It is so very far away, after all. Perhaps you will not like it there."

Montgomery shook his head to dismiss that possibility. "We will love it! We plan to travel as far to the west as we can go. People there are settling the land and making a new world! Life will be filled with adventure!"

He paused as they reached the corner most distant from the others and lowered his voice. "Dare I hope you will ever spare a thought for me, Miss Sterling, when I am far away? Will you think of me sometimes in the midst of your busy day?"

"Of course I shall think of you, Mr. Montgomery," she replied, smiling up at him demurely. "How could anyone who knows you fail to think of you and to hope that you—and your brother, of course—are being preserved from danger?"

"You are all kindness," he said, pressing the hand that rested upon his arm. He lowered his voice still more and said, "I cannot tell you, dear lady, how it would hearten me if you would allow me one of your lovely dark curls to carry next to my heart. Wherever I am, the memory of you would give me courage and a will to live."

"A curl?" she asked, touched by his request. "Why, yes, of course I will."

"You must cut it for me, and then we will arrange a time more private when you can give it to me without having to do so before the whole company," he said, his voice now a whisper.

Her heart beating rapidly, Ivy smiled her acceptance of his proposal. *An assignation!* she thought in excitement. She had not been wrong, then, in discerning a particular interest in her, no matter if the rules of politeness called for him to give his attention occasionally to others—like Miss Evans.

So absorbed had Ivy been in Mr. Montgomery that she had failed to note the entrance of her uncle and Miss Durrell. Her uncle was looking at Miss Durrell, but Miss Durrell, she saw at once, was looking at the two of them—and she could tell by a single glance the actress understood the situation at once. Ivy could not decide, however, whether that was comforting or unsettling.

Then she saw Mr. Westbrook was also observing them, and Ivy had no doubt about that. His gaze was decidedly unsettling.

Eight

For Ivy, the rest of the day passed in a pleasant blur. She knew herself to be singled out to receive Mr. Montgomery's particular attention, so it troubled her not at all when he sat down to a game of whist with Mr. Ravensby, Mrs. Rollins, and Miss Floyd. He looked up at her often, and it seemed to Ivy that his glances imparted volumes to her. Mr. Westbrook and Mr. Randall Montgomery sat reading, Miss Evans and the theatrical gentlemen were taking turns at a noisy game of beggar my neighbor, while Miss Durrell and her uncle sat talking quietly in a corner close to the fire. Her uncle had been forced to abandon his library after an avalanche of snow had drowned the fire, the weight of the heavy snow knocking out some of the chimney bricks.

Dinner was served to them in the saloon that evening, for her uncle had decided the dining room would be too drafty. Until further notice, he decreed only the yellow saloon, the kitchen, and the bedchambers would maintain their fires. Even those would be difficult to keep going, he warned, and they might have to reduce their number. The

others, having had a taste of cold rooms, agreed
that they could do very nicely with less space so
long as they had warmth.

After the dishes had been removed, she strolled
once more with Edmund Montgomery, and once
again they lingered in the remotest corner possible.
She waited eagerly for him to name a time and a
place for their meeting, but before he could do so,
they were interrupted by the rest of the group.

"All right, let us do this properly," said Miss Durrell, taking charge of the discussion, since Mr.
Ravensby was still cosseting his voice. "We have no
wish to spend the next few days playing cards—particularly when no one wishes to play for a pound
per point."

Here there was a brief murmur of agreement,
punctuated by bitter remarks by Mr. Jarvis and Mr.
Sneed about the parsimonious ways of some.

"And we have no desire to spend time in the ice-
coated billiard room nor in the snow-filled library
nor yet in the frozen depths of the dining room,"
she continued.

There was another, stronger murmur of approval
at this.

"Moreover, we know we are in need of amusement for the next two or three days until the
blizzard stops and the roads are clear."

Everyone nodded at the reasonableness of her
observation.

"So what are you thinking of, dear Miss Durrell?"
inquired Miss Floyd timidly, giving voice to the
question the others were thinking.

Miss Durrell smiled upon them, turning for a moment to gaze at Mr. Sterling, who appeared unable to look away from her.

"With the permission of our host, Mr. Sterling— dare I say, even with his blessing—we are to give a play!"

There was a brief pause as they all looked at each other, and then glanced about the room.

"Just how do you think we will do it, Div—I mean, Miss Durrell?" asked Mr. Sneed, changing his informality when he caught her eye. "I mean to say, here we are! How are we going to give a play in here?"

Miss Durrell shook her head in mock despair. "Honestly, Mr. Sneed, have you no imagination? We can clear the furniture to one part of the room and use the area just there"—here she indicated a swathe of space presently occupied by the pianoforte and the card tables—"as our stage."

Several of the others nodded their heads in agreement, and Mr. Jarvis sat down, deferring to her judgment. "But what will we present?" he asked. "And who is to be the audience?"

"If we must have an audience, Mr. Sterling has agreed we may use his servants. It would give them a pleasant break."

There was more nodding of heads at this, although some looked doubtful.

"And as to what we will present," said Miss Durrell, "considering we have with us young people and those who have never trod the boards, what better piece to present than one we all will know— *Romeo and Juliet.*"

There was a brief pause as they thought about it, but she took advantage of it to nail home her final point. "And our kind host, Mr. Sterling, has promised to sustain our efforts with a bowl of hot rum punch each night—just like the bowl Wheeling is bringing in now!"

This was greeted with a spattering of applause and great good humor. Wheeling directed the placement of the punch bowl, carried carefully by Gerald, and completed its preparation under the critical eye of the entire company. Then, amidst the toasts made by first one, then another—predominantly Mr. Jarvis— the group became more enthusiastic by the minute.

There were, however, exceptions.

Mr. Westbrook and Mr. Randall Montgomery took part neither in the rum punch nor the general air of celebration. Indeed, when Ivy was passed a cup of the punch, Mr. Westbrook removed it from her hand.

"You are taking too much upon yourself, sir!" she protested. "Pray leave me to take care of my own affairs."

"I would, if you would do so," he replied grimly.

"Miss Durrell, who will play Romeo?" inquired Mr. Finestone, looking hopeful. "I thought perhaps—"

"Mr. Edmund Montgomery is precisely the right choice," announced Miss Durrell, shattering Mr. Finestone's hopes. "He is of a suitable age; he is about to become an officer, so he is practiced in swordplay; and he has an excellent face, figure, and voice for the part."

"I thank you most gratefully, ma'am," said Montgomery, bowing low. "I shall do my best to rise to the level of expertise you and your company represent."

Here there was another general murmur of approval at this tactful speech.

"And who is to play Juliet?" asked Miss Evans, smoothing her hair self-consciously and glancing toward Edmund Montgomery. "I believe I may be the correct height for him, and certainly I am the most experienced actress."

"Which is precisely why you should not take the role," responded Miss Durrell briskly. "Juliet needs to be a very young woman, inexperienced in the ways of the world. And that is why the choice for our Juliet must be Miss Sterling."

Ivy was not flattered at hearing herself described in such a manner, but she was so delighted by the thought of playing Juliet opposite Edmund's Romeo that she could only smile. When Edmund looked meaningfully toward her, she thought her cup of happiness had indeed been filled completely.

It was just as well for Ivy she knew nothing of the conversation that followed hard upon the heels of Miss Durrell's announcement. Westbrook, singling out his host and drawing Sterling away from the others, muttered angrily, "Are you a damned fool, sir? What do you mean by allowing your niece to playact with a group such as this?"

Sterling straightened his shoulders and glared at this unexpected attack. "If I approve it, Mr. Westbrook, I do not see how a stranger such as yourself can question my decision."

"She is no more than a babe," Westbrook argued. "Who is to be her chaperone through all of this? She does not have even that protection, and she knows nothing at all of the ways of the world."

"If Miss Durrell feels it is proper for my niece to take part in the play, then it is proper," Sterling replied stiffly. "And knowing our circumstances as you do, how can you doubt she will always be in the company of others? My niece could not be safer."

Westbrook stared at him a moment, then shook his head. "You are quite hopeless," he sighed. "I hope it is not too late when you realize the foolishness of your decision. Do you not see your niece's interest in young Montgomery and his in her?"

"You take an inordinate amount of interest in my niece," said Sterling sharply, disregarding his remark about Edmund Montgomery. "Perhaps you would care to explain that, Mr. Westbrook."

"It appears to me someone should be looking after her," Westbrook replied. "She is both headstrong and innocent, and you do nothing to protect her because you are too absorbed in Miss Durrell."

"Perhaps that is the real problem," said Sterling suspiciously. "You are envious of my friendship with Miss Durrell, and you attempt to undermine it by conjuring up imagined problems."

Westbrook shook his head and turned away. "I wash my hands of the whole matter, sir. If you do not protect your own flesh and blood, then who can be expected to do so?"

"Not you!" said Sterling truculently. "I can take care of my own affairs."

Westbrook, seeing Ivy's eyes fixed on those of Montgomery, shook his head and turned away.

He found it infuriating that Sterling would not see reason, but he found it equally infuriating he himself felt any responsibility at all for Ivy's welfare. As he had told her earlier, he was not in the habit of considering other people, and he found this a most inconvenient time to begin to do so.

Taking everything into account, Mr. Westbrook found himself wishing devoutly he had ridden past Foxridge Hall and found shelter in some place far away from Miss Sterling.

Nine

The night was even colder than the day had been. At bedtime, people took their candles and reluctantly left the warmth of the saloon for the long, icy trek to their chambers. The ladies departed first, Ivy with MacTavish in tow, and the gentlemen next, with only one or two lingering in the saloon. Ivy had left orders for the fire to be kept burning steadily in that room for the duration of the night so that it would be a habitable place for breakfast the next morning—and, of course, for the beginning of their rehearsals.

Ivy, delighted by her role, had braved her uncle's displeasure to find a copy of the play on the bookshelves of his library. She had been poring over it whenever she had the opportunity, and she felt she already knew a substantial number of her lines. She did not prepare for bed that night, but sat before the fire reading the play and waiting for one o'clock to come. That was the time she had agreed to meet Mr. Montgomery in the saloon so that they might finally have the chance to speak privately. She had been made slightly uneasy by his proposal, but Miss Evans had joined them soon thereafter, clearly bent upon capturing Mr. Montgomery's heart.

That had been the deciding factor. If she were ever to have the opportunity to have a real conversation with him without being interrupted, she would have to take such a step as this. After all, she told herself, she was doing nothing so very wrong. Although she would be seeing him unchaperoned, it would harm no one, for no one would ever become aware of it. And if she did not, then the snow would thaw and Mr. Montgomery would leave without her ever having had the opportunity to speak with him privately. Obviously, she must take the opportunity that had presented itself.

When one o'clock came, she wrapped a thick shawl around her shoulders and stole toward the door, carrying her candle. When MacTavish left his basket to accompany her, Ivy shook her head.

"Stay, boy," she said quietly. "You can't come with me." She could not risk having Mac make a scene. Although she had told herself she was doing nothing wrong, Ivy did not wish to have to explain herself to her uncle and their other guests—particularly Mr. Westbrook, who was clearly expecting her to do something outrageous.

MacTavish stared up at her, disbelief in his expression and his stance. Ivy rarely left the room without him; the little terrier had become her faithful shadow.

"It's all right, Mac," she said comfortingly. "I won't be gone long, and you can come with me another time—just not tonight."

He sat down on his haunches and continued to stare at her, keeping his place until she had left the room and closed the door softly behind her. Then he stretched out, pressing his nose to the crack under the door so he could catch the last lingering scent of his mistress. He was unaccustomed to being left behind, and he was determined to wait by the door for her return.

Ivy, in the meantime, made her way down the shadowy passageway, her heart beating a tattoo. It was overwhelming, she thought, how different her life had become in a matter of just a few days. Bored to distraction, she had searched for something to do that would make her life more interesting. Most of all, however, she had been lonely. Now she had more companionship than she could deal with. And, of course, she appeared to have won the affection of Mr. Edmund Montgomery. Two nights ago, she never could have imagined that tonight she would be on her way to an assignation.

"Certainly I never would have believed it," she said aloud, watching the strange, flickering shapes cast by the candle. Smiling, she pulled her shawl more tightly about her shoulders and continued down the staircase. In her pocket lay a silky dark curl she had carefully clipped just minutes ago. He had pleaded with her once again today to allow him the talisman—just as he had asked her to call him by his Christian name. And how could she deny him, she thought, when he would be going into battle and had asked to be able to carry with him a token of her affection? His plea would have affected a heart far less impressionable than Ivy's.

She slipped quietly into the yellow saloon, moving quickly toward the fire, which she was pleased to see was leaping merrily. The room was still warm and welcoming. She had just placed her candle on a table and taken the curl from the pocket of her gown, when a slight movement caught her eye. There was someone seated in one of the high-backed chairs drawn close to the fire.

"Edmund?" she said softly, his name tasting honey-sweet on her lips. She moved lightly toward him.

"Robert," responded a voice far deeper than that of Mr. Montgomery. "I am sorry to disappoint you, Miss Sterling."

"Mr. Westbrook!" she gasped, the curl slipping from her fingers.

"I told you you would be disappointed," he observed, leaning over to pick up what she had dropped. He studied it for a moment, then returned it to her.

"Not at all," she managed to say, quickly tucking the talisman back in her pocket and carefully avoiding his eye. "You merely caught me by surprise, sir. Whatever are you doing down here at such an hour?"

"I found myself not at all weary, so when the others went up to bed, I decided to enjoy the fire for a while longer—particularly after one of the servants came in and added several logs to it. It seemed a pity to leave it for the cold walk to bed."

He eyed her speculatively for a moment. "Now it is your turn, ma'am. What brings you out of the warmth of your chamber on such a night as this?"

"Why, I merely wished to be certain the servants had indeed remembered to keep the fire burning brightly as I had asked," she replied glibly. "We would not wish to be greeted by an icy chamber at breakfast."

"Most certainly not," he agreed affably. "And, as you can see, they have done an admirable job. In fact," he added, picking up a book from his lap, "I believe I shall stay and enjoy it for a little while longer. I do not require much sleep, and this is a delightful place to spend my time. I would not be at all surprised if we were joined by others."

She stood there, staring at him helplessly. He was going to ruin her meeting with Edmund. She would not be guilty of so great an impropriety as going to his bedchamber or inviting him to hers, and there was no other place warm enough to meet.

"Will you not sit down, too, Miss Sterling?" he asked gently. "You have had a long day and are doubtless weary."

"No," she said dully. "Now that I know that all is well here, I must indeed go back to my chamber and rest."

He nodded. "Very wise. I shall remain here for another hour or two, I believe."

Ivy turned toward the door, bitterness flooding over her. She was certain he knew what she had planned and had deliberately thwarted it. "Good night, Mr. Westbrook," she said, a perceptible edge in her tone.

"Good night, Miss Sterling," he replied gently. "I trust you will sleep well."

And Mr. Westbrook did sit long before the fire that night, musing over the problem at hand and cursing the luck that had brought him to this particular house. He had problems enough of his own without adding the problem of a chit of a girl he scarcely knew.

Ten

Ivy scarcely slept at all that night, and she dressed and went down even earlier than usual to talk to Mrs. McGrundy. There was some comfort, she had found, to spending a little time in the warm kitchen in the presence of that bustling woman. This morning, however, Mrs. McGrundy had more grievances than usual to air, as she and Betty prepared to bake currant buns for breakfast.

"It's just as I told you, miss," she said darkly, kneading the bread as though she had the culprit on her bread board. "Some of the silver spoons have gone missing—three so far. I told Wheeling to count them every night, and it's a mercy I did, for last night he discovered I was in the right of it. He counted them twice over, but he come up three short each time."

Ivy could think of nothing to say to this—nor of anything she could do about it—but in an effort to divert the cook's thoughts, she said lightly, "Well, at least we haven't been murdered in our beds."

"Not yet," replied the cook briefly, slapping the dough as though it was behaving suspiciously. "Who's to say what will happen next?"

Having no answer for this, Ivy changed the subject completely. "Has it stopped snowing?" she asked, walking to the door to release MacTavish, who was waiting impatiently. Having the snow cease had become her greatest fear, for then Edmund would be leaving her.

Mrs. McGrundy snorted. "Not likely, miss. At this rate, it will be April before we can find our way out. My Sam says it's fortunate Mr. Sterling is a careful man and keeps a goodly stock of grain, or the horses would soon be too weak to pull a child's toy, let alone a coach."

"But he does have enough?" Ivy asked anxiously. "The horses will be properly fed?"

Mrs. McGrundy nodded with satisfaction. "Sam takes good care of his cattle. Even Mr. Westbrook, who is a most particular gentleman, has told him as much. Sam fair glowed when he told me what the gentleman said."

It was Ivy's turn for an unlady-like snort as she let in her dog and dried him. "Mr. Westbrook! He thinks far too well of himself!"

Mrs. McGrundy shrugged. "And so he should, miss. He's a proper gentleman, but he takes his responsibilities seriously. He goes out two or three times a day to see to his mount. Sam's that impressed with the care he gives him. Sam says Mr. Westbrook must leave as soon as it's possible to do so, but he don't want to risk his horse in such weather. He's going to leave him here with us and hire a mount from the stables at the Silver Parrot."

Ivy smiled. The fact that Westbrook would leave

as soon as possible was good news. Less pleasing, of course, was the possibility of his returning for his horse. It would be much more likely, however, that he would send a servant for it.

"Well, that will be one off our hands at any rate, Mrs. McGrundy. I daresay the others, since they are traveling by coach, will have to wait a little longer for the roads to be passable."

"No doubt they will stop long enough to pilfer all the silver," observed Mrs. McGrundy, still taking out her frustrations upon the hapless dough. "I should be glad to see them go and Mr. Westbrook stay. Why, that Mr. Sneak comes into my kitchen—"

"It is Mr. Sneed," interrupted Ivy gently.

The cook was unimpressed. "He comes into my kitchen just as though he has a right to do so. He acts as though he's here to take a look at the weather. He goes to the window, then over to open the door—"

"Fair freezes us out, he does, miss," added Betty, who had been listening earnestly as she worked.

"Says he needs a breath of fresh air," continued Mrs. McGrundy. "But then he peers about and asks if there's something a bit warmer than tea or cider to drink."

"Looking for spirits, he is, miss," contributed Betty, who had also clearly taken Mr. Sneed in dislike.

"And for the silver," said the cook. "And he's not the only one making himself at home back here where he don't belong. Why, that gangly young spider-shanks friend of his comes back here, too. Though he isn't looking for the brandy nor for the silver," she conceded, raising her eyebrows at the industrious little maid working beside her. "He comes back here to see Betty. I could see that from the first time he happened along here."

Betty turned scarlet. "Why, Mr. Jarvis is thinking no such thing!" she protested, but Ivy noted she looked mildly pleased.

Mrs. McGrundy shook her head at the little maid. "You mustn't even think about a playactor, girl," she cautioned her. "Everyone knows what they're like, and respectable folk must keep their distance from them—especially respectable young women."

It occurred to Ivy it would be better if she left the kitchen before Mrs. McGrundy became aware she was going to be involved with the actors in giving a play, for she had learned well enough in the past few days that the cook would not hesitate to deliver her opinion on the subject.

She turned to collect MacTavish, who had been enjoying a breakfast of porridge and milk, one of his favorite meals, at the hearth. The porridge, which coated his black whiskers and became rock-like when completely dry, had just begun to harden.

"Honestly, Mac," she scolded him affectionately, "could you not at least learn to wipe your own whiskers when you finish so I don't spend my life trying to make you look tidy again?"

MacTavish eyed her, unperturbed, and did his best to dry the damp whiskers she had just washed on the skirt of her gown.

"Don't scold him, miss. He's a good little dog—not nearly so much trouble as Mr. Sneak. In fact, I wish the dog would stay with us, for I noticed he don't care too much for the man. Barked at him, he did, when Sneak came back here and the dog was having his bone in front of the fire. Probably thought Sneak was going to try to make away with his bone—and he would, too, if he thought it was worth anything to him."

Seeing Mrs. McGrundy had once again launched into her favorite topic, Ivy excused herself and fled to the safety of the yellow saloon, hoping she would be able to think of some reasonable explanation for the play that would satisfy the cook.

She was amazed to find a flurry of activity in the saloon. Usually only Mr. Westbrook was an early riser, but this morning it appeared virtually everyone was in motion. Mr. Ravensby was overseeing the rearrangement of the furniture and was in the process of determining the stage area. He had posted Sneed and Jarvis as the markers for downstage left and downstage right, respectively, and was directing Mr. Finestone to move two chairs to indicate the corners of the stage area.

"I believe that will do," he said judiciously, surveying the scene as though he were planning a performance for the Earl of Lakeside. "It is a great pity, Frederick, that Miss Durrell did not consult me before announcing young Mr. Montgomery would play Romeo, for you, naturally, would play the role to perfection."

"And I should have had the part of Juliet,"

sniffed Miss Evans, who had been pouting ever
since the announcement had been made last night.
No one had noticed Ivy had entered the room.
"Certainly I have played it often enough. And
doesn't it say that Juliet is the sun? And isn't my
hair the right color for that?" she demanded of no
one in particular, tossing her corn-colored hair
over shoulder.

And it was, Ivy thought, just as well she was speaking to no one in particular, for no one answered
her, each being absorbed in his own thoughts.

"I, of course, shall play Mercutio," said Ravensby,
pretending to hold a rapier in his right hand and
lunging forward on his right knee to attack an
imaginary Tybalt.

"I don't believe that would be wise, Reginald,"
said Miss Durrell, who had quietly entered the
room behind Ivy. "I have considered the matter of
casting, and I believe that it would be best if I
played Mercutio."

Ravensby's chest and cheeks puffed up simul-
taneously, and Ivy reflected with amusement that
he looked precisely like a pigeon. "I believe,
madam, that I should make that decision," he said
pompously.

"Nonsense, Reginald," said Miss Durrell, ap-
proaching him briskly. "It requires too much
movement and too many sustained speeches. You
know Mr. Westbrook pointed out just yesterday that
your voice is suffering from the cold. What if you
should lose it entirely? You would not be able to
perform for Lakeside."

Reminded of their important engagement that had been delayed by the storm, Ravensby nodded reluctantly. "Perhaps you are right, Divina. I can see perhaps I should play—"

"The friar," inserted Miss Durrell neatly, before he could continue. "Undoubtedly, you should play the friar."

His expression revealed his disapproval clearly, but she continued unperturbed. "Where else could we find someone to play so virtuous a role without making him seem like a plaster saint?" she inquired. "Your ability will make him seem believable, and your presence on stage will give him a weight a lesser actor could not achieve."

His presence would certainly be a weighty one, thought Ivy in amusement, as Ravensby, puffed up even more by pride than he had been by indignation, strutted a little and struck what he apparently believed to be a thoughtful, virtuous pose. Miss Durrell's powers were formidable. Even someone like Ravensby, who knew her well and had watched her at work, fell prey to her honeyed words. No real enchantress from a fairy tale could have been more powerful.

Miss Durrell slipped her arm around Ivy's shoulders and said in a low voice, "You must not mind what Miss Evans said, you know. She is accustomed to playing Juliet, so it is a little difficult for her to give way to someone else."

Ivy nodded. "It is no matter. I only hope I do not make too great a mull of it so that everyone laughs at you for choosing me for the part."

Miss Durrell smiled. "You could not disappoint, my dear. You are lovely and young and have all the fresh qualities Juliet should have—including a young man who is in love with you."

Ivy stared at her, feeling the color rushing to her cheeks.

"Ah yes," said Miss Durrell, patting her cheek. "I could see at a glance how drawn you are to one another."

Before Ivy could respond, the actress lowered her voice still more and continued, "I do need to ask for your assistance, my dear."

"Of course," said Ivy earnestly. "How may I help?"

"Your uncle has had a fire made up in the book-room and has withdrawn to that chamber. He has told me he will take his meals there alone and re-main in seclusion until we all leave."

Ivy nodded slowly. "That is not surprising, Miss Durrell. My uncle prefers to remain alone, you see." She did not add that the only surprising thing was that he could separate himself from Miss Durrell.

"Yes, I have gathered as much. He is a most un-happy man."

"Unhappy?" asked Ivy, surprised. Such a thought had never crossed her mind. He was a most un-pleasant man, she was certain, but she had given no thought to the possibility of his being unhappy. "Do you mean he is unhappy because of all the people invading his privacy?"

Miss Durrell shook her head. "He has been un-happy for a very long time, my dear—since the time your parents married, in fact."

"My parents?" repeated Ivy, more startled still. "What do my parents have to do with his unhappiness?"

"He was, I think, very deeply in love with your mother—but she chose your father, his younger brother."

"He told you this?" asked Ivy, astounded both by what she said and by the fact that her gloomy, taciturn uncle would have told all this to a virtual stranger.

Miss Durrell once again smiled her slow, magical smile and nodded. "People often confide in me," she said, "gentlemen in particular."

Ivy had no trouble accepting the truth of what she said. She herself had succumbed to Miss Durrell's spell, so it required little imagination to believe a gentleman would. Not only did the lady make each individual seem special, someone apart from the crowd, but she had an uncanny ability to create trust, as though one could tell her one's deepest secrets. Ivy felt a sudden pity for her uncle, a lonely man with no one to love.

"But what do you wish me to do?" Ivy inquired, puzzled.

"I think you must look very like your mother did," said Miss Durrell gently. "I saw a miniature of her."

Ivy stared at her, more astonished than ever. "You have seen a miniature of my mother?"

"Your uncle carries it with him. I think seeing you must be painful for him."

Ivy nodded, remembering that he never did look

at her—and she had thought it was because he held her in dislike, not because the sight of her caused him pain. And he had indeed called her by her mother's name, Gwen.

"We cannot allow the poor man to remain in that bookroom, in the little prison he has created for himself," continued Miss Durrell. "He is distressed because I told him I could not keep him company there. He wishes me to forget about the play and spend my time with him."

Ivy had no trouble believing this. Of course her uncle would wish to keep Miss Durrell all to himself, far away from the company of others where they were so often interrupted.

"But, madam, there is nothing I can do to tempt him to come from his room!" Ivy protested.

"Ah, but you can, my dear. I wish you to go and tell him I would like him to play the part of the Prince in the play. There will not be a great many lines, but it is a most important role. And seeing you will serve to remind him he is still your guardian, and should be present to look after you."

"I do not need looking after!" declared Ivy mutinously. "Everyone appears to believe it to be so, but it is not. After all, I am of an age to marry."

"Yes, you are," Miss Durrell agreed. "I have told your uncle so."

"Have you indeed?" exclaimed Ivy, amazed by the news. "And what did he say?"

"He grew quiet, and said you are yet too young, whereupon I reminded him you could not stay here, isolated from the world, like Rapunzel in the tower."

Ivy was delighted. At last she had a champion, and a most formidable one at that. With Miss Durrell on her side, she felt as though there might be some hope of freedom for her.

"So, my dear, go and see your uncle, and beg him to come and act the part of the Prince for us," urged Miss Durrell. "Tell him"—here she glanced about the saloon and low laughter filled her voice—"tell him if he does not come, I shall be forced to send Mr. Jarvis down to keep him company in his lonely bookroom."

Ivy hurried down the passageway to the bookroom, her gown of scarlet merino doing little to keep out the icy drafts. Her uncle opened the door to her quickly, but his face fell when he saw her. She knew, of course, he had been hoping to see Miss Durrell.

Not waiting for his permission, she slipped past him to the fire, warming her hands in front of it.

"What brings you here?" he asked uncomfortably, pacing up and down the length of the little room without looking at her.

"I have a message for you, Uncle," she responded, rubbing her hands together and watching him from the corner of her eye.

He stopped abruptly and turned toward her. "A message?" he asked eagerly. "From Miss Durrell?"

She nodded, still not looking at him. "She wishes you to play the part of the Prince in the play."

She could see his shoulders suddenly slump. "Is that all?" he asked, sounding suddenly deflated.

"No," responded Ivy. "She says it is an important

part." She thought quickly, improvising a bit. "And she says she needs your presence, sir, for there is no one else in whom she reposes such confidence."

"Did she indeed?" he inquired, sounding more hopeful.

Ivy nodded, and finally turned to face him. "She appears to think very highly of you, Uncle."

He looked at her uncomfortably—but he did, she noticed, look directly at her.

"I suppose you think that an amazing thing," he observed.

She did, naturally, find it amazing, but decided it would be more tactful not to say so.

He nodded at her silence. "I have not behaved well, I know," he said. Then he looked at her more closely. "You are not involved with that young man, are you? The one who is to play Romeo?"

Ivy could feel herself flushing, but she held her temper in check. "How could I be, Uncle? All these people are strangers to us."

An uncomfortable silence fell as they both thought about what she had said. Both were well aware of how completely he had fallen under Miss Durrell's spell in so short a space, so the possibility of a relationship arising between herself and Mr. Montgomery was no less likely.

"Yes, of course you are quite right," he responded uneasily. "I don't see, however, how I can leave the privacy of this room for the bedlam of a rehearsal in the saloon."

"Miss Durrell has an answer for that, Uncle," responded Ivy, genuine laughter bubbling to her lips.

"Does she? And what would that be?"

"Why, she has promised to send Mr. Jarvis here to keep you company," she replied, her laughter bubbling over at her uncle's horrified expression.

"Why, then, by all means," he responded firmly, "if it is to be a question of Mr. Jarvis or the Prince, I have no choice but the Prince."

He was, she thought, almost human at that point, as he closed the door behind them and together they hurried back to the company of the others.

Eleven

When they arrived in the saloon, they saw that
rehearsal was in full swing. Mr. Ravensby was in-
structing Mr. Sneed and Mr. Jarvis and two other bit
players about how to conduct themselves as Capulet and Montague servants during the opening
scene, and Mr. Jarvis appeared to have countless
questions about the character he was playing. Miss
Floyd and Miss Evans were occupied in sorting
through the contents of two trunks Mr. Sterling
had ordered Wheeling to bring down from the
lumber room, Miss Floyd exclaiming over each new
discovery. At present she had a gaudily painted fan
she was exhibiting with pride to everyone.

"Perfect for the nurse!" she exclaimed triumphantly. "Is it not, Miss Durrell?"

Miss Durrell looked up to nod and smile. To Ivy's
surprise, the actress was deeply engaged in conversation with Mr. Westbrook, the two of them seated
close to the fire, but well away from the bustle of
rehearsal. Her uncle also noticed the couple and
he frowned, looking back at the door as though re-
considering his decision.

Hurriedly, Ivy found her copy of the play and opened to the Prince's first speech. "Here you are, Uncle," she said encouragingly. "You will have time to look over your lines for a bit before Miss Durrell talks to you about them."

"Yes, I suppose that's what she is doing now," he replied, brightening at the thought. "Probably taking Westbrook through his lines."

Ivy did not take issue with this, but she did not notice a book in the hand of either party. Nor could she imagine for a moment Westbrook would consent to taking part in the play. If Miss Durrell could convince him to do so, Ivy thought, she was an enchantress indeed. Nonetheless, the suggestion sent her uncle to pore over his lines.

Edmund Montgomery walked into the room just then, and his eyes lighted as he saw Ivy.

"I am so glad to see you, Miss Sterling," he said, taking her hand and bowing over it a moment before tenderly releasing it. He lowered his voice and leaned close. "I must apologize for failing to meet you last night. When I came downstairs, I saw Westbrook was still in the room, and I did not wish to draw his attention to us."

Ivy smiled at him reassuringly, although she was thinking wicked thoughts about Mr. Westbrook. "I understand," she said. "Your behavior was very discreet."

Mr. Montgomery looked relieved, his finely chiseled features relaxing a little. "We shall have to make other arrangements," he said. "Clearly the saloon will be off limits, since Mr. Westbrook keeps such late hours."

They were joined just then by Miss Evans, who managed to insert herself between them.

"Have you had the opportunity to practice your lines, Mr. Montgomery?" she asked. "I know them all by heart, and I should be most happy to rehearse them with you."

"You are all that is kind, ma'am," he returned, smiling his most winning smile, "but perhaps it would be best if Miss Sterling and I practice together."

Annoyed, Miss Evans flounced back to the trunk to help Miss Floyd.

"That was very thoughtful of her," observed Montgomery, watching Miss Evans try on a lace shawl. "Not everyone would be so generous with her time."

"Indeed not," replied Ivy, irritated by his obtuse comment. He had not even noticed Miss Evans had failed to offer the same help to Ivy. She was beginning to suspect the male was not the more astute of the sexes. "I was particularly struck by the way she offered to help me with my lines."

Recognizing the pique in her tone, Montgomery returned his attention hastily to her. "Let us find a quiet corner to practice together, Miss Sterling," he said, leading her to a corner far from the fire.

Giving way to her growing curiosity about the tête-à-tête between Miss Durrell and Mr. Westbrook, Ivy placed her hand on his arm and said, "Let's warm ourselves at the fire for a moment first, Mr. Montgomery I have not quite thawed from my journey down the passageway."

"Of course," he replied, leading her in that direction.

Together they stood at the fire, murmuring to one another in a low tone. Ivy strained to hear what she could of the conversation between Westbrook and Miss Durrell, but Mr. Jarvis soon joined them, and he was quite determined to talk over all the aspects of the play at a volume that could be heard in any corner of the room. Ivy abandoned Mr. Montgomery to carry on the conversation and devoted her attention to eavesdropping without appearing to do so. Happily, the loud monologue delivered by Mr. Jarvis provided an umbrella of protection, for it would not seem anyone within earshot could hear anything save him, so the two on the nearby sofa continued their talk without fear of being overheard.

"Yes, I can understand how trying that must be to a man of your disposition," Miss Durrell was saying comfortingly, her liquid voice balm for any wound, "but you must remember she is a very young woman."

Ivy, thinking they were speaking of her, bristled immediately, but she kept her gaze studiously upon the leaping flames of the fire.

"Nonsense, Miss Durrell!" snapped Mr. Westbrook. "Youth is no excuse for being a fool!"

Miss Durrell laughed her lovely, golden laugh. "Indeed, sir, it is often thought the only excuse for being one."

He laughed reluctantly. "Perhaps so," he admitted. Ivy was astonished. She had never heard him admit to being wrong about anything. "But I am certain, dear lady, you have never been such a fool."

Certain now that they were speaking of her and irritated beyond belief that he thought her a fool and Miss Durrell a saint, Ivy could scarcely keep herself from whirling upon them.

"You are too kind to me, I fear," replied Miss Durrell. "I have been a fool many times and doubtless shall be so often again."

"I would never believe it possible, ma'am," he replied gallantly, and from the corner of Ivy's eye, she could see him raise the lady's hand to his lips and kiss it.

Forgetting her own response to Miss Durrell, Ivy thought bitterly that the way men made fools of themselves over her was quite disgusting. Westbrook certainly had no business thinking anyone else a fool when he was proving himself one as well. She was thinking of turning to point that out to him when the conversation continued.

"So what will you do about her?" inquired Miss Durrell, and Ivy was immediately all attention.

"Why, I shall forbid her to make the match, of course," he responded quickly. "I have every right to do so!"

Ivy's jaw dropped. She knew him to be an interfering, overbearing, mannerless man, but this exceeded anything she could have imagined. How, she wondered indignantly, could he possibly think that he had any right to forbid her to make a match? If she wished to marry Edmund Montgomery, she would do so! Provided, of course, she amended hastily, that Edmund asked for her hand.

"That scarcely seems wise," demurred Miss Durrell, "for you must know when a young woman is forbidden to do something, that is precisely what she wishes most to do."

Reluctantly, Ivy conceded Miss Durrell was alert upon every count. Mr. Jarvis increased his volume once more so it was difficult to hear, and it was all Ivy could do to keep from turning around and pulling up a chair to join the couple behind her. She had to content herself with straining to hear every word.

"Even though I am quite in my dotage," continued Miss Durrell, "I must confess if you were to say such thing to me, I should feel compelled to marry the man out of spite."

Ivy, torn between her desire to applaud Miss Durrell's sentiment and her annoyance at the observation that she was in her dotage, clearly intended to make Mr. Westbrook deny such a possibility, waited eagerly to hear his response.

"I suppose you are quite correct," he admitted slowly. "I suppose much of this is because my pride was hurt when she cried off."

This was almost more than Ivy could bear. Mr. Westbrook wasn't speaking of her after all. The young lady he spoke of had broken her engagement to him!

The momentary surge of pity she felt for him was lost in a new wave of Mr. Jarvis' monologue, and from the corner of her eye, she could see Miss Durrell patting his hand comfortingly. So Mr. Westbrook, of all people, had been sent to the right about! She could scarcely take it in. Judging by what Miss Durrell had said, the young lady to whom he was engaged was a very young lady indeed. Without a doubt, this was the urgent business he needed to attend to in London.

Just then Mr. Ravensby called them all to attention, informing the group that the servants were ready to introduce their portion of the play, followed by a scene featuring Romeo; Benvolio, played by Mr. Finestone; Tybalt, played by Mr. Westwood, further astonishing evidence of the powers of Miss Durrell; the Prince, played by her uncle; Montague, played by Mr. Ravensby; and Capulet, also played by Mr. Finestone after a hasty change of jacket. Spurred into action by this announcement, there was a brief flurry of activity, and Ivy heard no more of the conversation between Westbrook and Miss Durrell. Still, she found herself watching that gentleman covertly and wondering about his fiancée. She was annoyed to discover she almost felt some sympathy for the man, despite his lack of manners and his habit of thinking too well of himself.

Soon, however, she had no time to spare a thought for anything except the play and Edmund Montgomery. To her delight, Miss Durrell insisted upon rehearsing the scene when Romeo and Juliet first meet at the party before any of the other scenes.

"It is too important a scene to leave until last," she said firmly, overriding the protests of those who were involved in the earlier scenes. "Once we have

We'd Like to Invite You to Subscribe to Zebra's Regency Romance Book Club and Give You a Gift of 4 Free Books as Your Introduction! (Worth $19.96!)

If you're a Regency lover, imagine the joy of getting **4 FREE Zebra Regency Romances** and then the chance to have these lovely stories delivered to your home each month at the lowest price available! Well, that's our offer to you and here's how you benefit by becoming a Regency Romance subscriber:

- 4 FREE Introductory Regency Romances are delivered to your doorstep (you only pay for shipping and handling)

- 4 BRAND NEW Regencies are then delivered each month (usually before they're available in bookstores)

- Subscribers save almost $4.00 every month

- You also receive a FREE monthly newsletter, which features author profiles, discounts, subscriber benefits, book previews and more

- No risks or obligations...in other words, you can cancel whenever you wish with no questions asked

Join the thousands of readers who enjoy the savings and convenience offered to Regency Romance subscribers. After your initial introductory shipment, you receive 4 brand-new Zebra Regency Romances each month to examine for 10 days. Then, if you decide to keep the books, you'll pay the preferred subscriber's price, plus shipping and handling.

It's a no-lose proposition, so return the FREE BOOK CERTIFICATE today!

Say Yes to 4 Free Books!

Complete and return the order card to receive this $19.96 value, ABSOLUTELY FREE!

If the certificate is missing below, write to:
Regency Romance Book Club
P.O. Box 5214, Clifton, New Jersey 07015-5214
or call TOLL-FREE 1-800-770-1963
Visit our website at www.kensingtonbooks.com.

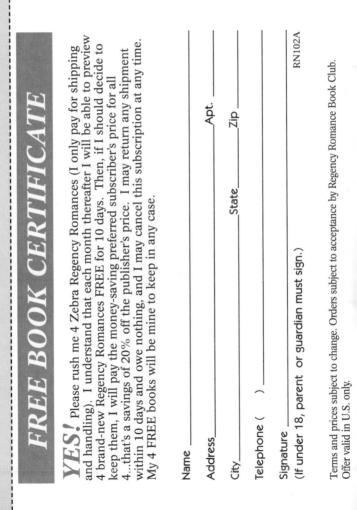

FREE BOOK CERTIFICATE

YES! Please rush me 4 Zebra Regency Romances (I only pay for shipping and handling). I understand that each month thereafter I will be able to preview 4 brand-new Regency Romances FREE for 10 days. Then, if I should decide to keep them, I will pay the money-saving preferred subscriber's price for all 4...that's a savings of 20% off the publisher's price. I may return any shipment within 10 days and owe nothing, and I may cancel this subscription at any time. My 4 FREE books will be mine to keep in any case.

Name _____

Address _____ Apt. _____

City _____ State _____ Zip _____

Telephone ( ) _____

Signature _____ RN102A
(If under 18, parent or guardian must sign.)

Terms and prices subject to change. Orders subject to acceptance by Regency Romance Book Club. Offer valid in U.S. only.

been through this once, Miss Sterling and Mr. Montgomery will need some time to practice on their own while we are working on other scenes."

"But Romeo is needed in some of those scenes, too," complained Miss Evans, who was to play Lady Capulet.

"We can use a stand-in for him in those," replied Miss Durrell. "Their first meeting is the vital scene for them to rehearse."

There was still some muttering over this, but she blithely ignored it, telling all of them where they should be positioned for the opening of that scene. In the midst of the bustle, Westbrook firmly steered her to a private corner for a conference.

"You will do splendidly as Tybalt," said Miss Durrell approvingly, patting his muscular arm appreciatively. "I daresay you are no stranger to swordplay yourself, Mr. Westbrook."

He eyed her appreciatively. "Much as I would like to discuss such matters with you, ma'am," he returned, "I fear what I wish to say is that you should not allow Miss Sterling to play a role like this."

"Like Juliet?" Miss Durrell demanded, her delicate brows arched in surprise. "Why ever should I not?"

"You know quite well it is not suitable for a young woman like her, not even out of the schoolroom yet, to be playing a romantic role with a strange young man in a group of—" Here he paused delicately.

"In a group of tawdry actors?" she inquired dryly. "Well, now that you have put it so tactfully, I can naturally see your point, sir."

"You know full well what I mean, ma'am," he

replied, not to be diverted from his purpose. "What is acceptable for Miss Rosa Evans is not acceptable for Miss Ivy Sterling."

"Indeed? Miss Sterling is, I would point out, not a schoolroom miss. She is a young lady of an age to be married."

"Which is precisely why this should not be taking place," retorted Westbrook, holding his irritation in check with some difficulty. "She has no more sense than a peagoose, and no one to take care of her who has any more wit than she does! Any sensible man would be put off entirely by such behavior as she is being allowed to exhibit! How will she find a husband who will have her?"

"It appears Mr. Edmund Montgomery would be quite interested," replied Miss Durrell. "I am merely providing the opportunity for the two of them to become better acquainted."

"What absolute rubbish! He's not about to take a wife, as you very well know! He's going off to war!"

"Delightful though I have found our conversation, Mr. Westbrook," said Miss Durrell, turning away from him, "I fear I have other responsibilities to see to at the moment. The players await me."

To his profound annoyance, she once again began to arrange the actors and smiled gently at Ivy, patting her cheek.

"Do not look so worried, my dear," she said soothingly. "You will do wonderfully well."

Westbrook's first inclination was to leave them all and return to his room, but remembering that the fire in his room would not be replenished until bedtime, he moodily decided he would stay where he was. In fact, he found when he was called upon to say his lines, he could glare at Romeo quite effectively and deliver his threat against that young man with a convincing snarl before storming from the stage.

"Bravo, Westbrook!" cried Miss Durrell approvingly. "You have made it very believable that Tybalt will challenge Romeo to a duel to avenge this insult."

"And so I will!" snapped Westbrook, still glaring at Montgomery.

"Now you see, everyone, if we can all play our roles with the same fervor Mr. Westbrook does, we shall have a most convincing production."

Westbrook retired moodily to a corner by the fire, wondering if he would have a sword for the fight scene with Romeo and Mercutio. He felt quite convinced he could use it effectively. In fact, instead of merely cutting down Mercutio, he felt he might be able to alter Shakespeare's play somewhat and run Romeo through as well.

"Fools!" he muttered, glaring at all the other players. "If they put all their wits together there would not be enough for one sensible man!"

Miss Durrell, he was quite certain, had her own reasons for placing Ivy in such jeopardy. He found the actress appealing, but he was in no danger of succumbing to her charms. Far more practiced, more elegant flirts had tried to take him in. She was, he was quite certain, thinking of the vulnerable Mr. Sterling and the very handsome Foxridge

Hall. It would be far easier for Miss Durrell to become mistress of the manor if she had disposed of the niece.

He tapped his nail thoughtfully against his teeth, thinking of the knotty problem at hand. He had not stopped to ask himself why he was so concerned about a matter that was really none of his affair. He was, he told himself, merely confronted by a situation he could not ignore for the simple reason he could not leave this house or this group of people. And he was, after all, a man of conscience and of reasonable good sense.

His gaze darkened as he saw Mr. Jarvis bustling about to prepare for the balcony scene. *Fools!* he thought to himself bitterly. Alistair Sterling was paying not the slightest heed to his niece, who was clinging to Edmund Montgomery's arm. No, Sterling was staring down into the golden eyes of Divina Durrell. Not a sensible one in the group.

"Mr. Westbrook?"

Torn from his thoughts, he looked up to see Mr. Randall Montgomery looking at him hesitantly.

"I must apologize, Mr. Westbrook, but I overheard a little of your conversation with Miss Durrell, and I believe we share a similar concern."

Westbrook stared at him for a moment, then indicated a chair near him. "Please, Mr. Montgomery, I would like to know what you are thinking. I was afraid no one else saw this situation as a problem."

Randall Montgomery, a slender man with a sensitive, likeable face, seated himself carefully and drew his chair closer to Westbrook.

"It is indeed a problem," he agreed. "I know you are worried about Miss Sterling," he said in a low voice. "I am also concerned about her, and I am equally concerned about my brother."

Westbrook nodded encouragingly. After a considerable pause, Randall Montgomery began to talk, and Westbrook leaned toward him, listening intently.

"I hesitate to share my brother's affairs with anyone else," he said slowly, "but I had not anticipated encountering such a situation as this before we left to take part in the war in North America."

He paused and Westbrook watched him impatiently, fighting the urge to bark at the gentleman. He could see Montgomery was laboring under considerable emotion. "Edmund has always been mercurial—a little unstable in temperament. Charming, too, of course," Montgomery added hastily. "You can see that."

Westbrook did not find Edmund Montgomery at all charming, but he could see that others did, so he nodded without comment.

"Edmund has always needed excitement," he continued, "and he has sought it in various ways. He rides well and he loves to race and to hunt and—"

"And to gamble?" Westbrook added, remembering the episode in the billiards room. If the room had been warm enough for them to remain there for any length of time, he was certain young Montgomery would have been playing for very high stakes—or at least as high as his company would allow.

His brother nodded reluctantly. "And I am afraid your concern for Miss Sterling is not unfounded. Edmund is not always reliable in his behavior with ladies."

"And does that have something to do with his becoming a lieutenant and leaving the country?"

Again Mr. Montgomery nodded. "There were earlier escapades when Edmund was little more than a boy—one with a married woman, one with a young woman of questionable reputation—but our father managed to deal with those discreetly. Just recently, however, Edmund eloped with a young woman of good family and considerable fortune."

"What happened?" demanded Westbrook. This was far worse than he had bargained for.

"Her father and I overtook them before they reached Scotland, and we managed to cover up the matter. I knew he had no real interest in being married. He was only creating excitement for himself, and I realized he would continue to do so. I would never have been able to watch him closely enough to keep him from disaster, so I resigned my living and made arrangements for Edmund's commission. Now he will have real adventures to occupy him—and the military may provide some of the discipline he needs."

The two men sat quietly for a moment, considering the problem.

"He would prefer to be with Wellington, of course," added Mr. Montgomery, smiling wanly, "but I felt America would be a better choice. Once the war is over, we will very likely sell out, and then we will be living in a society with a frontier and adventures that suit a man of his disposition. I think he may be able to find a place for himself there more readily."

"And you believe you can keep him out of trouble until you get him to his regiment?" asked Westbrook.

Mr. Montgomery shrugged ruefully. "I had thought I would be able to do so. I had not counted upon this storm, nor upon finding ourselves in such close company with a young woman of Miss Sterling's charm and beauty. This is a most unfortunate situation."

"That is an understatement," responded Westbrook grimly, staring across at the players. "We will not get any of the others, even Sterling, to listen to reason and help us to keep them apart. Even if you told him what you have just told me, he would dismiss it."

"Then what can be done?" asked Montgomery in despair. "Even if the storm were to stop this moment, we could not travel immediately. And the closeness of our situation means they must always be together, even if there were no play."

"The play may be a better thing than I had thought, given the circumstances," Westbrook conceded reluctantly. "At least if they are saying their lines, they are under everyone's eye, instead of spending their time together in more private conversation."

"So you believe all we can do is to keep our eye upon them?" Montgomery asked.

"We will also talk to the two of them," replied Westbrook. "You will speak with your brother, and I will speak with Miss Sterling. We have no one to rely upon except ourselves, since her uncle will do nothing and Miss Durrell refuses to assist us."

"But will it do any good to talk to them? Edmund certainly does not always attend to what I say to him. What if they will not listen to us?" asked Mr. Montgomery, looking far from reassured by this plan.

"Then we will think of something else," responded Westbrook firmly.

Twelve

While the two gentlemen were talking, the rehearsal was progressing. Mr. Jarvis and Mr. Sneed had worked out a makeshift balcony by dragging a heavy table onto the area marked as the stage. Mr. Edmund Montgomery helped Ivy climb to the tabletop, and the rehearsal continued, with Mr. Montgomery staring up at her worshipfully and Miss Evans watching them darkly. Things could not be better, Ivy thought with satisfaction, giving herself to the pleasure of the moment.

After they had managed to get through the balcony scene successfully, Ivy excused herself to go to the kitchen and check upon matters there. In a brief whispered conversation before departing, she promised to meet Edmund in the bookroom in just a few minutes. Her uncle and Miss Durrell were deeply engrossed in conversation, so the young lovers felt their meeting place would be a safe one.

Ivy found Mrs. McGrundy and Betty hard at work in the kitchen, and she could see at a glance something was weighing upon the cook's mind. She was uneasily certain of what it was.

"Is something troubling you, Mrs. McGrundy?" she inquired lightly.

The cook shook her head, not glancing up.

"Perhaps you have heard we are giving a play in order to pass the time," Ivy remarked, stooping to pat MacTavish so she had something to do with her hands and felt a little less awkward.

Mrs. McGrundy nodded, still not looking up from her work.

"You mustn't be concerned about me, for everyone is there, including my uncle," ventured Ivy, daunted by this unusual silence. Since Miss Willowby's departure, Mrs. McGrundy had been the only person she had talked with, and she knew that lady had grown fond of her.

"It's not my place to say anything, miss," the cook reproved her.

"We needed something to do, you see," Ivy said, trying once more. "We could not have a dozen people just sitting there, staring at one another for hours on end."

"Playacting!" sniffed the cook, beating the batter in the large bowl ferociously.

"It is all very innocent," Ivy reassured her, hoping her cheeks were not betraying her. "Indeed, it is almost like doing my studies with Miss Willowby, for I am reading Shakespeare."

"And what was he but another actor, miss, and one who wrote for actors, to boot?"

If Ivy had hoped to lend respectability to their undertaking by the mention of Shakespeare, she could see her attempt had been wasted. If anything, the cook thought rather less of the Bard than of mere actors. After all, he supplied them with their lines. She clearly felt without riffraff like him, actors could not exist.

"Six spoons," said Mrs. McGrundy succinctly.

"Six spoons?" repeated Ivy, startled by the abrupt shift in subject.

The cook, however, made the connection clear. "Wheeling counted the spoons again last night and found three more missing. That makes six spoons what has been stolen, miss! Six! Soon you'll have nothing to eat with!"

Ivy did not want to think about missing spoons, for her thoughts were all with Edmund. Having managed to calm Mrs. McGrundy somewhat by promising to watch the actors carefully when they ate, particularly Mr. Sneak, she slipped out to hurry to the bookroom.

To her delight, she found Edmund waiting for her—alone—when she arrived. She left the door ajar as she entered, thinking that would be more discreet, but Edmund came over and closed it behind her.

"You will be letting out all of the warm air, dear lady," he told her, drawing her closer to him and closer to the fire. "I would not wish for you to become ill because you have come out in the cold to meet me."

She smiled at him tenderly. He was so kind to her, so concerned for her welfare, she thought happily. A very different sort of man from most, she told herself.

Shyly, she took the lock of hair from her pocket and slipped it into his hand.

"How lovely," he said softly, holding it carefully and stroking its silky length. "Now I will always have a part of you with me, no matter how far away I am or how desperate my situation."

"I will think of you always," she assured him earnestly, looking into his eyes, "but if I were with you, there would be no need to rely only upon a lock of hair."

His eyes widened slightly at that, but he nodded. "I can think of nothing more wonderful than having you by my side," he assured her, drawing her close.

"It would be wonderful, wouldn't it?" she agreed softly, allowing him to embrace her. "Neither of us would have to be alone."

"That has been my dream," he murmured, his breath gently moving the tendrils beside her ear. "Our lives would be twined together."

"That is just what I was thinking," she said, delighted by his observation. "More than anything, I wish to take care of you."

He took her hand and pressed it to his lips, holding her closely to him. "You are more than I deserve," he murmured, "much more."

Before she could demur, another, less tender, voice said, "Yes, I would say she is much more than you deserve, Mr. Montgomery. She is also much more than you will receive. Perhaps you should go back to your chamber with your brother and think about that. The icy air there might help to clear your mind. Or you might discuss the matter with Mr. Sterling. I am certain he would be interested in your thoughts about his niece's well-being."

"Mr. Westbrook!" she exclaimed, outrage causing her to shake uncontrollably. "How dare you eavesdrop and interfere in a matter that is none of your concern."

"I'm afraid you're wrong, Miss Sterling," he replied. "Although I didn't want this to be my concern, I see that it has become my business. You should have one adult with common sense to look after you. Your uncle is far too involved with Miss Durrell to make rational decisions on your behalf. All he can see is Miss Divina Durrell."

Although privately Ivy agreed with him wholeheartedly, she could not bring herself to say so when he had once again chosen to insert himself into her business without any invitation to do so.

"Your interference is really unforgivable, Mr. Westbrook," she informed him sharply. "Mr. Montgomery and I do not need your advice, no matter how valuable you reckon it to be."

"What about it, Mr. Montgomery?" replied Westbrook. "Would you like me to summon Mr. Sterling so that you can explain all of this to him?"

"There's no need to call my uncle," Ivy announced angrily. "All that would bring about is greater confusion than we have right now. He has no interest in my activities."

"Perhaps you should leave us, Mr. Montgomery," said Westbrook, opening the door wide for him. "Your brother is waiting for you in the passageway, and I need to speak with Miss Sterling for a moment."

Before Ivy could protest, Edmund strode out of the room, not glancing back at her. Westbrook closed the door firmly behind him and turned to look at her.

"How dare you behave in such a high-handed manner, sir." she fumed. "Open that door, if you please, so I may leave, too!"

As she started past him toward the door, Westbrook stepped in front of her. "I cannot let you go, ma'am, until I have spoken with you."

"Nonsense!" she retorted, still trying to move past him. "I shall not stay!"

"Indeed you will, ma'am," he said, looking down at her and placing his hands firmly upon her shoulders so she could not move. "You leave me no choice but to stop you forcibly, for you must hear what I have to say."

MacTavish barked warningly, standing as close to his mistress as he could, but Westbrook ignored him.

"I can see that you fancy yourself in love, Miss Sterling, but—"

"I do not fancy it! I *am* in love, and Edmund loves me!"

"Does he indeed?" replied Westbrook, still holding her firmly and still trying to ignore MacTavish, who was now growling ominously, teeth bared. "Has he told you so?"

"Not yet," she was forced to admit, "but he will do so soon enough. He might have said so just now, had you left us our privacy!"

"And even if he does tell you that," Westbrook continued brutally, "what are those words worth from a young man who longs for adventure? You merely provide him with a brief dalliance, like the other young women he has left behind him."

"You are lying," Ivy retorted, but with less certainty. "How could you know such a thing?"

"His brother told me as much," Westbrook replied.

Ivy was infuriated to realize a tear was slipping down her cheek. "You are a horrid man!" she exclaimed, pulling away from him and turning back toward the fire so he could not see. "It is no wonder your fiancée cried off! Any young woman of good sense and good taste would do so to avoid being paired with a man like you!"

There was a brief pause as she stared into the fire, waiting for his reply.

"You may be quite correct," he said finally, measuring his words. "I may indeed be a horrid man and the young lady you speak of may have been quite justified in her decision, but that does not affect your own situation."

"Oh, but it does, sir!" she exclaimed sharply. "You are unhappy, and so you are determined others shall not be happy. I daresay you are as jealous of our happiness as it is possible to be."

"Jealous?" he repeated in disbelief, his dark eyebrows rising. "Of Montgomery?"

"Of our happiness! Ours would not be a marriage of convenience like your own was to be!" she said, turning back to face him once more, her tears under control. "You cannot bear to see a young couple happy when you have been jilted yourself! I daresay you are jealous of my uncle and Miss Durrell as well. Perhaps I should warn them to beware of your wicked tongue!"

Ivy marched past him and out of the room, followed closely by the equally indignant MacTavish, who made a final snap at Westbrook's boots in passing.

Randall Montgomery had had no better luck with talking to his brother. He and Westbrook compared notes in the yellow saloon.

"Edmund was all righteous indignation," Montgomery sighed. "He told me he had done nothing amiss and that he is indeed deeply in love with Miss Sterling. Then, in high dudgeon, he asked me if I thought they were about to run away together, and, if so, just how I thought they would do so in the midst of such a storm." Montgomery shrugged and stared into the fire. "And I had to admit he had a point there."

A moody silence ensued as the two watched the rehearsal, once again under way under the supervision of both Miss Durrell and Mr. Ravensby, who were busily giving conflicting instructions to the actors. Mrs. Rollins was holding forth as the nurse, and Miss Evans looked suitably bored as Lady Capulet. Ivy and Edmund, seated close to one another on a sofa, appeared to be going over their lines together.

"I believe, Mr. Montgomery, it is time to take

other measures," said Westbrook. "Miss Sterling spoke to me of jealousy, and I believe jealousy might be the very tool to separate her from your brother."

Randall Montgomery looked at him hopefully, and Westbrook proceeded to explain. It would take very little, he knew, to reawaken Miss Sterling's jealousy of Edmund Montgomery's association with any other young woman. All he needed to do was to arrange a scene that would do so. Thoughtfully, he eyed Miss Evans and Miss Durrell, wondering which of them would best suit his purposes.

Thirteen

"Come now, Miss Sterling, do show a little more emotion, please," said Miss Durrell. "After all, this is your dear cousin Tybalt who is dead. Try it again. And do sound sorry that he is dead."

Ivy glanced at Mr. Westbrook, who was lounging against a nearby chair, looking distinctly—and, Ivy thought, regrettably—alive.

"'O God, did Romeo's hand shed Tybalt's blood?'" she cried to Mrs. Rollins, swathed in a voluminous gray gown as her nurse.

"'It did, it did, alas the day, it did!'" that lady lamented in return.

"Much better, much better!" applauded Miss Durrell.

"Pray don't stop her there, Miss Durrell," called Westbrook. "Should she not go on with the speech denouncing Montgomery—I mean, Romeo?"

Ivy darted a venomous glance toward him, but Miss Durrell nodded, so she proceeded with her speech. "'O serpent heart, hid with a flow'ring face! Did ever dragon keep so fair a cave?'" she began, looking intently at Mrs. Rollins so she could block out any view of Mr. Westbrook. She could not, however, block out his voice.

"I have often found, Mr. Jarvis, that life is very much like the theater," he observed audibly, and Mr. Jarvis nodded in quick agreement.

Before Mr. Jarvis could give voice to his agreement, however, Westbrook continued quickly, "How often we find someone who appears to have every virtue—just as Juliet feels about her handsome Romeo—only to find precisely the opposite is true."

"Just so," nodded Jarvis. "Often I've said something on stage that has given my stomach a queer turn because I knew it was the truth." He paused a moment thoughtfully, then added, "O' course, sometimes that was because I had et my supper just before performing, a habit which is to be avoided whenever possible. Generally, I have just a biscuit and tea."

"Mr. Westbrook and Mr. Jarvis, you are disturbing the actors," Miss Durrell reproved them. "You know quite well you should not be standing so close and talking while they are delivering their lines."

Before they could go on with the rehearsal, Ivy turned again to Mr. Westbrook to observe tartly, "I have found what you say is quite accurate, sir. There is often truth in literature."

"I am pleased to hear you agree with me, Miss Sterling," he said, bowing briefly, "although I must confess I am surprised by your admission."

"I was thinking particularly of the attempt of Paris to marry so young a lady as Juliet," she continued. Westbrook had been called upon to play both Tybalt and Paris. "That seems to me very much like real life—an older man attempting to force a much younger lady to marry him. Does it not seem familiar to you, sir?"

After smiling at him sweetly, she turned back to Mrs. Rollins and Miss Durrell to continue her scene.

At the close of that scene, Westbrook walked over to her and bowed. "You are growing very quick, ma'am," he observed lightly, an unaccustomed smile creasing his face. "You turned my remark to your advantage very neatly."

She curtseyed. "I was pleased to be able to do so, Mr. Westbrook. I do promise to give you pleasure in that way whenever I may."

"Yes, I am certain you will," he agreed. "And I shall look forward to it."

He watched her with appreciation as she strolled away from him. It was a thousand pities she should try to throw herself away upon such a man as Edmund Montgomery, who had nothing except his handsome face and figure to recommend him.

He continued to meditate upon that problem as he made his way out to the stable to check upon his horse. At least he could be grateful that the cattle were well cared for at Foxridge Hall.

In the kitchen he greeted Mrs. McGrundy and Betty, then made his way carefully to the stable. He was still using the rope, as were the others who had to make the journey back and forth. The snow had grown lighter today, but the wind was still a problem, whipping around the corner of the Hall and blinding the wayfarer with blasts of white.

"Would you like a mug of cider?" inquired Mrs. McGrundy when he arrived back in the kitchen, shaking the snow from his beaver hat and his coat and boots. They had established a pattern by this point, and he nodded affably.

"Indeed I would, Mrs. McGrundy," he told her. "I have never had better cider at any posting inn in the country."

She beamed at him as she handed him the tankard, which she had already prepared for him. He made himself comfortable on the settle in front of the fire, which had become his favorite place in the house. There he sat two or three times a day, thawing from the cold, drinking cider, and chatting with the cook. He looked up at her and grinned, prepared to begin another serious conversation about the merits of mulled wine and jugged hare, food and drink being their favorite topics of conversation. A glance at her expression stopped him, however, for her smile had faded and she looked quite serious.

"Is there something amiss, Mrs. McGrundy?" he asked.

"Begging your pardon, sir," she said reluctantly, "I know I'm speaking out of turn, but—"

"Nonsense. What seems to be the problem?"

"You are a gentleman, sir, as is my master, but there are others in the house who are not."

He nodded. "That is true, ma'am."

"It is Miss Sterling I worry about, sir, since she has no lady to look after her since Miss Willowby left us."

"Miss Willowby?" he inquired.

"Her governess," replied the cook. "When it was just us here at the Hall, it was not so bad, although I know it was lonely for the young lady, but now—well, now, it's different. She needs a lady to keep her company."

"I could not agree with you more, Mrs. Mc-Grundy," he said grimly.

The cook's expression eased a little at this. "Do you think she will come to any harm with this group of playactors, sir?" she inquired a little timidly. She could not believe she was saying such things to a gentleman, for she never would have dared to say them to Mr. Sterling. Mr. Westbrook, however, had an easy manner, and she knew how highly her husband Sam thought of him.

"I will see to it," he assured her, rising to turn his back to the fire as he finished his cider. "She will be quite safe, Mrs. McGrundy."

"Thank you, sir," she said gratefully. "You have eased my mind. I couldn't think of anyone else I could turn to to help the young lady."

"She is fortunate to have you, ma'am," he said, smiling at Mrs. McGrundy. "For you are quite in the right of it—she does need looking after."

Relieved that she had done the right thing, Mrs. McGrundy returned to her work, and Westbrook walked thoughtfully back to the yellow saloon, laying his plan for the evening.

Dining had become a very informal affair since they had confined all of their activities to one drawing room. The servants brought in the food on trays and placed it on a massive sideboard that Gerald and three other men had moved into the room, and the dishes and silver and glassware were also placed on the sideboard so that the guests could serve themselves with ease. Then they all found themselves places to sit and held their plates on their laps.

"It is quite charming—almost like dining *al fresco,*" Miss Floyd had twittered upon the first occasion.

"If we were dining *al fresco,* we'd already be frozen solid," Mr. Sneed had observed, edging closer to the fire.

On this night, Westbrook noticed the party seemed more subdued than usual, possibly because the storm seemed to have reasserted itself, and the wind was whistling at the windows and down the chimney so that everyone was shivering a little, even those closest to the fire. Mrs. Rollins had her fur muff, from which she removed her hands only when eating, drinking, or playing cards. Little Miss Floyd was wrapped in two shawls, her old thin one and over it the handsome cashmere shawl Ivy had insisted upon giving her.

"Perhaps a little music would improve our spirits," suggested Mr. Westbrook when dinner was over.

"I'd say the hot rum punch would do us more good," observed Mr. Sneed, who stood with his back as close to the fire as he dared without setting himself ablaze.

"Mr. Sneed!" said Miss Durrell reprovingly. "You must remember we are guests of Mr. Sterling!"

"Yes, well, I believe Mr. Sneed may be quite

correct," said Alistair Sterling, who was feeling the cold himself. "I will have Wheeling bring it in earlier than usual tonight."

This brought about a murmur of approval, and again Westbrook said, "While we are waiting, a little music would do us good. As I recall, Miss Evans, you have a charming voice. Would you sing something for us?"

Pleased to be singled out, even though the pianoforte was rather closer to the windows than she would have liked, Miss Evans moved to the instrument with alacrity. Ivy noticed with irritation that each time the young lady came to the chorus of her ballad, she gazed directly at Edmund Montgomery when she sang the words "Dearest love, what shall I do when you are gone?" And, she noticed, Edmund seemed captivated. Not once did he turn to gaze at Ivy as those tender words were sung.

Pleased with the success of this attempt, Mr. Westbrook urged Miss Durrell to favor them with a number as well, and that lady's honeyed notes soon filled the room. For a few minutes all of them were caught in the warmth of her voice, and their cold and the whistling winds were forgotten. Even Ivy forgot to glance at Edmund. Not until Wheeling and Gerald appeared with the punch bowl was the spell broken.

With the advent of the punch, there was a bustle of cheerful activity, and Mr. Jarvis began to rehearse the healths he intended to propose. Ivy, moving quietly to Edmund's side, was annoyed to find that Miss Evans had arrived there first and that everyone was discussing the possibility of the troupe visiting North America once the war was over. Edmund was disgustingly enthusiastic about it, she thought.

"Just imagine," he was saying to the others, as Miss Durrell and Mr. Ravensby listened thoughtfully, "you could bring your troupe of players and tour the towns and cities in Canada and America. They would flock to see you."

"Yes, I believe I can see it," said Ravensby, looking up as though the scene floated somewhere close to the ceiling of the saloon. "We would be feted by all those who hunger for the theater and the sound of their mother tongue."

He tossed his head and posed, preparing himself for the crowds that awaited him.

"Will they want English actors after the war?" asked Miss Floyd timidly. "Canadians would, of course, but perhaps the Americans would object to us."

"Nonsense," responded Edmund. "Most of the Americans are against this foolish war, and it will be over with in a matter of a few more months. Then they will be eager to see English actors."

"Certainly they have no culture of their own," observed Ravensby. "We shall be missionaries, carrying the English stage to them."

Mr. Jarvis raised his cup and cleared his throat. "To our pair of young adventurers who are braving the seas to go to the other side of the world and help to end a war," he trumpeted, looking at the Montgomery brothers.

The rest of the company raised their cups. "To the adventurers," they chorused, drinking deeply.

"And to the talented troupe that will show America what the theater really is," said Edmund, raising his cup and smiling.

The others once again chorused and drank. By the time Wheeling and Gerald had thrice replenished the punch bowl, the group was quite convivial and no one was feeling the cold. The long walk to bed, lighted by their candles, was less of an ordeal than it normally was, and it seemed to them that even the wind was dying down.

It was not, however, the end of the evening.

When Ivy arrived in her chamber, she found a note upon her pillow, written in a strong, masculine hand. It instructed her to wait for half an hour after everyone had come upstairs to bed, then to return to the bookroom. Smiling, she sat down beside her fire with MacTavish to wait for her tryst.

Downstairs, Westbrook, still awake, waited patiently in the shadows outside the yellow saloon to see the fruits of his labors. The first to appear was Miss Evans, her candle lighting her way to the bookroom, where Westbrook had thoughtfully left candles burning.

Soon came Edmund Montgomery, moving softly down the passageway and pausing at the door of the saloon, as though tempted to stop in and see if Mr. Westbrook was still there. Next came Ivy, moving softly and quickly, anxious to meet her lover once again. Westbrook was grateful she had not brought MacTavish. He had counted upon that, for the little dog would have betrayed his presence immediately.

Ivy opened the door to the bookroom gently and slipped inside. Before she could close it, however, she looked up and gasped. Edmund was standing in front of the fire, but he was not alone. He was embracing Miss Evans.

At the sound of her quick intake of breath, they separated and looked up, Miss Evans triumphant, Edmund sheepish. In his hand he held a long yellow curl, obviously belonging to Miss Evans.

"Miss Sterling!" he exclaimed. "I thought you had asked me down here to meet you."

"I can see you were expecting me," Ivy replied coldly. "Forgive me for intruding."

And she turned back to the passageway, closing the door behind her.

Westbrook, who was watching at a distance, silently applauded her. She had handled herself well, not allowing her distress to show. She had come very far in just a few days, he thought, no longer betraying her every emotion.

However, as she passed, he could hear her sob, and he was momentarily sorry he had arranged this whole affair. Still, he told himself, even though it was a painful lesson, it was a necessary one if she were to be protected. She would not believe Edmund Montgomery would betray her unless she saw it with her own eyes. Now she had seen it.

It had been a necessary cruelty, he told himself again, trying to forget the sound of her sob.

He returned to the yellow saloon and he sat long before the fire that night.

Fourteen

Whether as a result of the rum punch or their weariness or the cold—or perhaps a combination of the three—no one rose early the next morning. Indeed, by the time most of the group had gathered, the morning had almost passed.

"Well, if Miss Sterling would make her appearance, we could proceed with rehearsal," observed Miss Durrell. It was time for the scene when the lovers part, and Edmund Montgomery had been going over his lines with Miss Evans.

"Perhaps she isn't coming down this morning," remarked Miss Evans brightly. "She may have the headache, and I could take her part."

Mr. Westbrook looked at her with dislike. Rosa Evans was not a pretty young woman. She had only youth and a luxuriant mane of yellow hair to recommend her, and just now her smugness made her particularly unappealing. He felt Edmund Montgomery deserved her.

"If she isn't well, perhaps one of us should look in upon her," said Miss Floyd, her thin face wrinkled with concern. "I could go up, if you like."

"You're very kind, but that won't be necessary, Miss Floyd," Alistair Sterling assured her. "My niece may well be consulting with the cook and have lost track of the time. I will send Wheeling to look into the matter."

After responding to the bell, Wheeling moved slowly toward the door to send other, younger servants to look into the problem. It was clear the unaccustomed exertions of the past few days had taken their toll on the old man's strength.

In the interval, Edmund and Miss Evans continued their practice, while Miss Durrell rehearsed Mr. Sterling's lines with him. Mr. Ravensby was once again growing reflective over his sausages, and the others were either finishing their breakfasts or warming themselves in front of the fire. Once again the wind was howling and the snow was whirling down. Mrs. Rollins pulled back the heavy velvet curtain over one of the windows, but the others exclaimed loudly against the sudden blast of cold air and, even more chilling, the sight of the storm.

"Look at that!" exclaimed Jarvis, who had moved closer to the window. "You can't see anything out there except for white!"

"We'll not be leaving today, that's a certainty," said Sneed, turning his back on the sight.

"We are so fortunate to be here where it's warm!" exclaimed Miss Floyd. "Just think how dreadful it would be to be caught out in that!"

"We would be dreadfully dead," agreed Sneed, returning to the fire.

Mr. Westbrook had been idly watching the others,

hoping Miss Sterling was not truly in bed with a headache to avoid facing her problem. He would be very disappointed in her after the manner in which she had handled herself last night. He had already been out to the stable, and he had reassured Mrs. McGrundy everything was well in hand. He did not like to be wrong.

Suddenly the door opened and Wheeling came hobbling in with unaccustomed speed. He made his way quickly to his master, and there was a sudden flurry activity in that corner of the room.

"What is it? What's to do?" demanded Westbrook, striding over to Alistair Sterling.

"Wheeling says Ivy has gone!" he said starkly, his face white. "But that cannot be true. Not in this storm. She must be in the Hall somewhere."

"What of her dog?" asked Westbrook. "Was he in her room?"

Wheeling shook his head, his lined face taut with worry. "The chambermaid said the dog wasn't in his basket beside the fire when she went in this morning, but she thought nothing of it. She thought Miss Sterling had taken the dog into the bed with her, and the bedcurtains were pulled tight against the cold. But her cloak and boots are gone and the bed was not slept in."

Alistair Sterling and Wheeling went to the kitchen to organize the servants for a search inside the Hall, and Westbrook sent all of the guests scurrying through the parts of the Hall they knew, all of them calling for Ivy and MacTavish, then listening hopefully.

After an hour of intensive searching, there had been no sign of either of them. Mr. Jarvis had manfully braved the snow, clinging to the rope to make it to the stable and back again, but no one there had seen Miss Sterling or her pet. Mr. Jarvis had reported his tidings while standing in front of the kitchen fire, flanked by the admiring Betty, who had brought him a mug of cider.

Westbrook cursed himself for a thoughtless fool. All of this had undoubtedly happened because of his little trick last night. The child had not been able to handle the disappointment; she was too young for such a blow. The same thought appeared to have occurred to Edmund Montgomery, for he looked unusually grim, and even Miss Evans was less smug. If the child had gone outside in this storm, her fate was certain.

After pacing the saloon and periodically jerking back the curtains to peer outside, Westbrook took himself back to the kitchen. Mrs. McGrundy was preparing supper, but tears were coursing down her cheeks as she worked.

"I told her we'd be murdered in our beds by the playactors," she told him, turning to check the rabbits roasting on the spits, "but I never believed she would be the one lost."

"Come now, Mrs. McGrundy, Miss Sterling isn't missing because of the actors," he assured her. "And what you told her had nothing to do with what has happened to her." He thought bitterly that he knew just where the blame rested.

"Miss Sterling is a sensible young woman," he

said, trying to convince himself. "Perhaps we may still find her."

"Do you think so, sir?" the cook asked, willing to trust someone that was telling her what she wanted to hear and who was—apparently—better equipped to judge such matters.

"Think hard, Mrs. McGrundy," he urged her. "Is there any place in the Hall where she might be? Is there a priest's hole or a hidden passageway or entrance? Any place she might go to be alone?"

He had asked Alistair Sterling the same questions, but he had assured Westbrook no secrets of the Hall were unknown to him and they had searched every hiding place possible. Sometimes, Westbrook knew, the servants knew what their masters did not.

But Mrs. McGrundy shook her head slowly, thinking through everything she knew about the Hall and about Ivy. "Outside of the stables, the only other place she goes is the gatehouse—and she can't go there in weather such as this."

"The gatehouse!" he exclaimed, seizing upon it. "Does she go there often?"

"Oh, yes sir," replied the cook. "I know she does, although she don't talk about it. Miss Willowby didn't want her to go there, but Miss Sterling likes to go down and watch the road from the top of the wall. She and the tyke would go inside and build fires and have their tea. Sam told me that because he saw the firewood was being used, so he chopped up some more and left it for her. He thought the young lady should have a place of her own."

The gatehouse! Westbrook thought furiously, remembering the day when he had arrived. She and the dog had been going somewhere away from the Hall in all that snow—undoubtedly to the blasted gatehouse. Now how was he to find it in the midst of this storm?

"Mrs. McGrundy, how far would you say the entranceway of the Hall is from the gatehouse?" he asked.

The cook looked at him blankly, and he said patiently, "Look at my stride, ma'am." Here he walked about the kitchen. "How many steps do you think it would take me to reach the gatehouse?"

She looked at him helplessly and he patted her shoulder. "Never mind, ma'am," he told her, looking about the kitchen. His gaze alighted upon Gerald, who had been watching him intently.

"Come here, man!" he commanded, and once again he took several steps. "How many steps do you think it would take me to reach the gatehouse?"

Gerald's eyes closed and he appeared lost in thought, his lips moving. "Perhaps five hundred, sir," he replied.

"Good man!" exclaimed Westbrook, patting the footman's shoulder. "And when I leave the front entrance of the Hall, do I walk straight ahead?"

Gerald again closed his eyes, as though to picture the scene, then shook his head. "You go a little to the east, sir—but not very much."

"Very good!" repeated Westbrook, again slapping his shoulder. "Your master should raise your wages! Now bring me all the rope you have!"

Gerald and the other footmen hurried to bring every coil of rope they could find, and Westbrook had them knot the pieces carefully together.

"It's not enough to reach the gatehouse, sir," cautioned Gerald when they had finished.

"It's enough for a start," replied Westbrook, sounding more confident than he felt. This was the only thing he could think of to do. Gerald would knot the rope at the main entrance to the Hall, and Westbrook would follow it for as long as he could, walking in the direction Gerald had indicated. When he ran out of rope, he would drive a stake into the ground and fasten the rope to it, with a length left to pull above the drifting snow. To this he would tie the long red woolen scarf Mr. Jarvis had been wearing for warmth.

All of the others watched the preparations anxiously. Darkness was almost upon them again, and they had little hope Westbrook would make the journey successfully.

"That's no more than three hundred feet of rope," Sneed observed in a low voice to Jarvis as they watched them knotting the pieces together. "That won't get him to the gatehouse."

All the others, including the servants, gathered in the Great Hall as Westbrook prepared to leave. They bid him farewell as they would have one who was never to be seen again.

"Thank you, Westbrook," said Alistair Sterling in a low voice, pumping his hand before he left. "I should be going instead of you, but I know I could not do it. I hope to God you can, sir."

"So do I," replied Westbrook, grimly.

"Just a moment, sir!" called Mrs. McGrundy, just as they had opened the door and he was about to plunge out into the storm. She had come puffing from the kitchen, her arms filled with packages. "Excuse me, sir," she said, slipping them into the pockets of his greatcoat.

"What are you doing, Mrs. McGrundy?" demanded Sterling in irritation.

"Those are venison pasties, hot from the oven," the cook told Westbrook, ignoring her master. "Their heat will keep you warm, and you will need something to eat when you get to the gatehouse. God bless you, sir!"

"Mrs. McGrundy, if you weren't married, I would marry you the instant I returned," he said, kissing her on the cheek.

A moment later he was gone, his figure disappearing into the whirling whiteness. Bleakly the little group stood there for a few minutes, but realizing there was little they could do, they drifted forlornly back to the yellow saloon to await the morning. Only Gerald stayed by the entrance, opening the door now and then to be certain the rope still held.

It seemed to Westbrook he had walked for hours before he reached the end of the length of rope. He had tried to concentrate on nothing save counting off the steps and holding his direction. If he allowed his mind to wander, he knew all would be lost. He could not allow himself to think Ivy might not have made it to the gatehouse, that she might have lost her way in this storm and lie frozen somewhere in the drifts close beside him. There was no profit in thinking of that, only defeat. And she did, after all, have the small beast with her. That gave her a decided advantage, he told himself as he patiently marked off the steps, trying to keep his bearings. Darkness was falling quickly, and soon he would run out of rope. Then he would have to struggle on with only good fortune and his sense of direction to guide him.

When he came literally to the end of his rope, Westbrook bent to shove the stake he had carried in his pocket into the ground. It went in more easily than he had expected, and he pulled the length of rope tied at its end above the drifts and knotted Mr. Jarvis's scarf about it. Then he laid it carefully across a drift that reached almost to his shoulder. He knew that the large damp flakes would probably turn the red scarf totally white by morning, but this was the best he could manage.

Now rudderless without his rope, he set his course firmly and placed his faith in Gerald's estimate. Carefully he counted out his steps, concentrating so that nothing would cause him to lose track of them. Soon he told himself that, if Gerald were correct, he would have twenty more steps to take. As he paced off the last of them, he caught a glimmer of light through the falling snow. It was indeed the gatehouse!

Feeling his way around the house, and remembering where Gerald had told him the door was, Westbrook at last felt the door and its latch! Triumphantly, he swung open the door.

"God bless Gerald!" he exclaimed, stepping into the room in a blast of wind and snow.

"Mr. Westbrook!" exclaimed Ivy, recognizing his voice and jumping up from her place by the fire. "How ever did you get here?" Taking a second look at the man she would scarcely have known because he was so coated by snow, she added, "Are you frozen, sir?"

"I am indeed, Miss Sterling!" he exclaimed, staggering toward the fire. "Damn and blast, I am indeed! And I am relieved to see you are not."

MacTavish, who had risen from his place beside the fire at the opening of the door, watched the stranger without a sound.

"What, not barking, small beast?" inquired Westbrook, holding his frozen hands toward the fire. "You must not be well."

Here he turned toward Ivy. "Are you not taking care of your dog, Miss Sterling?" he demanded. "Why doesn't the little beast bark at me?"

"He must think you an apparition, sir, as I do," she responded, still staring at him. "However did you come here, Mr. Westbrook?"

"Painfully, Miss Sterling, very painfully," he replied, trying to peel off his gloves. He discovered, however, that his fingers did not seem inclined to work, and he had to relinquish that duty to Ivy, who carefully removed them and then rubbed his hands briskly with her own.

"What are you doing here?" she asked again. "You could have lost your way and died, sir. Have you no common sense?"

He stared at her for a moment, blinking his eyelashes to clear some of the snow that clustered upon them. "I must admit, Miss Sterling, you do not disappoint me," he observed. "Most young women would swoon or perhaps even throw themselves into my somewhat frozen arms because I had come to save them. You, however, question my good sense."

"Well?" she said impatiently. "Naturally I would. I did not need to be saved, so why would you come out in such a storm?"

"The same question might be asked of you, ma'am!" he retorted. "Why did *you* come out in this storm?"

"When *I* came out early this morning," she replied tartly, "there was a lull in the snow and the wind. *I* did not take my life in my hands. I simply did not wish to be at the Hall any longer, in so much company, so MacTavish and I came out here."

"Without leaving a message for anyone?" he demanded. "Did you believe we would know where you had gone and that you were safe? We have been searching for you for hours! You hen-witted chit, how could you leave so many people to believe you lost?"

"I did no such thing," she replied hotly, turning away from him to the fire. "I left a note for my uncle, telling him I was coming here and he should not worry about me. I knew I would have no problem reaching the gatehouse."

"And where did you leave this note?" he inquired. "We certainly did not find it."

"In his bookroom," she replied. "I placed it on the desk. I thought that the most likely place for him to find it since he cannot use his library."

"Oh," replied Westbrook. It was perfectly true he had not been to the bookroom that morning, and he was fairly certain Mr. Sterling had not either. Both had been late coming downstairs, and both had remained in the warmth of the saloon. "I don't believe he received it. We thought you were lost, you see."

She nodded grimly. "You made that perfectly clear when you called me a hen-witted chit!" she retorted.

"Well, you must grant I had seen you lost in a storm before, running about in the snow with no pelisse or cloak! And as to being a hen-witted chit, what would you call yourself?" he demanded, incensed. "You left the Hall in the midst of a blizzard because some young man with more hair than wit had upset you!"

"Really?" she asked, her voice suddenly cold. "And just how would you know a young man had hurt me, Mr. Westbrook? I don't recall mentioning that to you."

Fifteen

Chagrined by his slip, he noticed even the dog seemed interested in his answer. MacTavish peered up at him searchingly, and Westbrook gave his attention to the dog rather than Miss Sterling, for the terrier seemed slightly less forbidding. The young lady was standing poker-straight, and he could see from the corner of his eye she was waiting for him to look at her.

"Well, sir?" she demanded. "What made you say such a thing to me?"

"As a matter of fact, Mr. Montgomery mentioned the matter to me after you left!" he retorted, trying to ignore a stab of conscience as he turned to face her.

"Edmund told you about what happened?" she asked, her eyes darkening in disbelief as she looked at him.

"I believe you interrupted him during a tête-à-tête with Miss Evans," he responded stiffly, trying to tell himself he was being truthful about that at least.

"Yes," she sighed, looking away from him at this

indication he knew the truth. "Edmund was telling her the same things he had said to me, and he had a lock of her hair, just as he had asked for a lock of mine. I would not have believed it possible if I had not seen it with my own eyes."

She sank down on the settle, which had been drawn close to the fire, and placed her face in her hands. MacTavish leaped up beside her and nosed at her gently, whining softly in sympathy. Ivy did not look up, but she tucked her arm around him and pulled him close.

"Yes, I understood something like that had happened," he said uncomfortably. "But you mustn't let it upset you, Miss Sterling."

"Indeed?" she remarked, her voice muffled. "And why must I not?"

He paused a moment, a little puzzled by her question. "Why, because he is not worth the trouble, of course," he responded.

Ivy lifted a tear-stained face to stare at him directly. "And why is he not worth it, Mr. Westbrook?" she demanded.

Westbrook stirred uncomfortably. "Because he has no scruples about engaging your affections," he responded uneasily. "Because he treats you just as he would any other feather-witted young girl he would meet."

"I believe it was hen-witted," she observed, blowing her nose.

"Well, it's all the same!" he replied testily.

There was a sudden silence, and he realized she was studying him. He was careful not to meet her eyes, and he tried to appear unaware of the examination he was undergoing.

"No, it is not!" she said abruptly. "And I did not think he was treating me as he treated other young women. I still cannot believe what I saw!"

Here she attacked him directly. "But why do *you* think he should not treat me just as he would any other young girl, Mr. Westbrook? What possible difference could it make to you?"

"Because you are not just any young girl!" he responded in irritation. "Certainly you know that, Miss Sterling!"

"How would I know it?" she asked simply. "My parents thought me someone special, of course, but they were my parents. After I lost them, no one else told me I was. Why should I think it?"

"Because it is true and because you are able to think!" he exclaimed, annoyed. "You should have arrived at that conclusion on your own!"

"Even with you assuring me at every turn that I am a hen-witted chit?" she inquired. "That is scarcely an observation that would improve my opinion of myself."

"Your opinion of yourself should not hang upon what I or anyone else says about you, ma'am! In spite of what I said, I thought you were more clever than that, but perhaps you are just a pretty widgeon after all!"

They glared at one another for a moment. Then, before Ivy had an opportunity to reply, Westbrook abruptly sat down beside her on the settle. The exertions of the past few hours had suddenly made themselves felt.

"Much as I would like to continue this brangling, Miss Sterling," he sighed, stretching out his feet toward the fire, "if you will forgive me, I must rest for a moment."

Almost before he could finish the sentence, his eyes had closed, a wave of warmth and exhaustion overcoming him. Ivy struggled with her annoyance for a moment. How typical, she thought, that he should have the last word and then cut off her opportunity to respond by going to sleep.

Nonetheless, she reminded herself he had, after all, come searching for her through the storm. She looked at him, defenseless now, already snoring gently, and she felt a stab of remorse. What he had done, he had at least done out of concern for her.

It took her several minutes' struggle to remove his greatcoat, for it had become sodden in his journey, and she tucked blankets around him as he slept. In the pockets of the greatcoat she found Mrs. McGrundy's pasties and smiled, heating supper for herself and MacTavish.

After they had eaten, she lifted the dog onto the settle, placing him between herself and Westbrook and tucking the covers around them all.

"He is a peculiar man," she told her dog, who thumped his tail in agreement, "but he was, after all, willing to come after us through all of this storm. So perhaps he is kinder than I had thought him—even though his manner leaves much to be desired."

When Westbrook awoke in the morning, he came to with a start. He knew he was cold and in an unfamiliar place, but it took him a moment to get his bearings. Then he realized he was not alone. His arm was wrapped firmly around Miss Sterling's shoulder, and she was leaning against him, her forehead no more than an inch from his lips. The fire had burned low, and the room was filled with shadows. Her face, however, caught what light there was, and seemed to glow against the darkness.

Almost without thinking, he bent closer and kissed her lightly. A growl and a sudden movement reminded him of MacTavish's presence. The dog was wedged between them, and he did not accept Westbrook's sudden movement graciously. Growling, the terrier wriggled out from under the blanket and looked at Westbrook indignantly.

"What's the matter, Mac?" murmured Ivy sleepily. Her hand slipped out from under the covers, and she reached out as though to pat her terrier.

Her hand encountered Westbrook's cheek and her eyes flew open.

"Good morning, Miss Sterling," he greeted her, his eyes no more than an inch from her own.

He could see her rapidly thinking through what had happened, trying to remember the course of events, but he did not allow himself to smile. After all, he had awakened a few minutes earlier, so he had the advantage.

"You came to find me," she said at last, staring at him.

He nodded, pulling her closer, folding his arm about her, and kissing her firmly. He knew that, for a moment at least, she yielded. Then he felt her stiffen and pull away from him.

Irritated, he opened his eyes. She was looking him squarely in the eye.

"Well, ma'am?" he said impatiently.

Ivy stared at him for a moment before replying. "Why did you really come here, sir?" she asked.

Caught off guard, he allowed himself to stare back. "What do you mean, Miss Sterling? I came here to find you, of course, just as I told you."

"Yes, but why did you come, rather than any of the others?" she demanded. "My own uncle did not come, nor did the young man who had made me believe he loved me. Only you. Why?"

Overcome with irritation, Westbrook realized she had him. "Because I felt some responsibility for your situation!" he said abruptly, sitting up straight and pulling farther away from her.

She studied him closely. "But why should you have?" she inquired, patting MacTavish. "How could you possibly be responsible?"

He could not bring himself to look at her, but he decided he would have to make a clean breast of things. His pride would not allow him to lie.

"Because I left the notes in the bedchambers," he responded. "One for you, one for Miss Evans, one for Mr. Montgomery."

She looked at him in astonishment. "You left the notes? But why, Mr. Westbrook?" she asked. "I cannot imagine why you would trouble yourself with such a matter."

Still he could not bring himself to meet her gaze,

although he could feel it. "Because I was certain Edmund Montgomery was not in love with you," he replied. "I was certain he would take advantage of you just as he had of other young women."

"And you thought that it would be good for me to see that," she mused, saying it aloud as though talking to herself. Then her tone hardened. "What you did was cruel, Mr. Westbrook!"

"No, ma'am, it was not!" he said, turning finally to look into her eyes. "It would have been cruel to let you believe him and to abandon a young girl like you to his pretty speeches. Forcing you to see the truth about him was the kindest thing I could do!"

"Was it indeed?" she returned, looking at him.

"Yes," he said simply. "How could I let you believe a lie?"

"And you were responsible for Edmund meeting with Miss Evans," she added, still staring.

Again he nodded. "You are worth thirty of him," he murmured, leaning over and kissing her forehead lightly. It was so easy to do, he thought, such a natural thing. She was so close—and he wished to kiss her.

"And so you came through the storm for me," she repeated, ignoring his kiss. "You came because you felt guilty—and so you should have! Edmund would not have been meeting Miss Evans had you not arranged it!"

She pulled away from him and sat looking into the fire. "You told her to cut a lock of her hair, didn't you?" she demanded. "You had seen the curl

I had cut, and you thought my seeing her with Edmund, handing him a lock of her hair, just as I did, would break my heart!"

Before he could answer this unexpected attack, she turned back to him, her words barbed. "I was correct when I said you are cruel—so you are! Cruel and arrogant, making decisions about other people's lives without a thought about whether or not you have the right to do so!"

She stood up and pulled on her cloak.

"Just what do you think you're doing, Miss Sterling?" he demanded, trying to ignore the justice of her accusation.

"I'm going back to the Hall to see Edmund!" she responded grimly. "He cannot help it if young women like Miss Evans insist upon throwing themselves at his head. She would not have been there to meet him had you not interfered. I love Edmund Montgomery, and I shall marry him, too!"

"If you are paperskulled enough to marry him, Miss Sterling, then I shall wish you joy. You will deserve whatever befalls you!" he snapped.

"You really are insufferable!" she gasped. "I could almost be sorry for you because your fiancée no longer wishes to marry you, but your behavior makes me feel she was most fortunate to avoid the connection!"

"I begin to see she was very kind to save me from the parson's mousetrap," he responded. "Indeed, your behavior makes me grateful I have been spared the company of any young woman."

Ivy fastened her cloak firmly and pulled up the

hood. "I'm going to go back to the Hall to try to undo some of the damage you have done, sir!"

"Then you will wait for me so you don't die on your way back there, ma'am! It is astounding to me you were not dead long before this if you make a habit of using so little common sense in your decisions."

"And if I cared for your good opinion, I would be crushed," she responded, pulling on her gloves and reaching for MacTavish. "But as it is, I am quite unmoved by your comment."

She almost reached the door ahead of him, but he managed to arrive first and take charge of the situation. He opened the door carefully, having to push against the snow that had drifted against it, and he leaned out to look for Mr. Jarvis's red scarf. To his amazement, he caught a glimpse of it, even though the snow was still falling.

Together, the three of them set out, Ivy carrying MacTavish and following Westbrook closely as he tried to retrace his steps from the night before. To their great relief, he found the scarf and the stake, so they followed the rope safely back to the Hall, their silence as cold as the icy weather. Gerald, who had been waiting faithfully, flung open the door immediately and helped them into the Great Hall. The others, summoned from the saloon by Wheeling, hurried to greet them. Even the servants, headed by Mrs. McGrundy, hovered in the background, eager to see the wayfarers safely home.

"I cannot thank you enough, sir!" exclaimed

Sterling, pumping Westbrook's hand. "You have brought my niece home safely!"

Ivy stared at him in amazement. "Why would you be so grateful, Uncle?" she inquired. "You haven't paid a particle of attention to me in the year I have been here."

He nodded. "I know you are correct, Ivy," he told her. "And just look at what almost happened because of that! How could I ever have looked myself in the eye again if my lack of care had been responsible for your death?"

To Ivy's astonishment, he did indeed look anguished, and he went so far as to pat her arm and to stoop to pat MacTavish.

The others crowded around them in welcome, even Edmund and Miss Evans, who both looked somewhat conscience-stricken.

"No need, Edmund," Ivy whispered to him when he tried to stammer an apology. "It does not matter now. It was not truly your fault. I will explain to you later what happened."

As Miss Sterling started wearily up the stairs toward her chamber, accompanied by MacTavish, Miss Durrell, and Miss Floyd, she had the satisfaction of seeing that Edmund followed her every movement with his eyes, ignoring Miss Evans, who was clinging to his arm. Westbrook, his dark hair still crusted with snow although he had removed his hat, was also watching her, but Ivy did not spare him a glance.

Sixteen

Westbrook also retired to his chamber, eager to wash in the hot water Gerald had promised to bring immediately. He felt he was very likely frozen to the core, and he longed to wash in front of a crackling fire, put on some dry clothes, and take himself downstairs for breakfast. He did not add, even mentally, that he wished to go downstairs so he could see Miss Sterling again—nor that she obviously had no wish to see him.

When he strolled into the yellow saloon, he was surprised to be greeted by a round of applause.

"Take a bow, Mr. Westbrook!" said Ravensby, surging toward him, hand outstretched. "You are the hero of the moment and have given a fine performance. We are all indebted to you for bringing Juliet safely home."

"But why'd she go out in weather like this?" asked Mr. Jarvis wonderingly. "Had her dog gone missing during the night?"

Sneed snorted. "I told you last night, Jarvis, no one would risk his neck for a dog! Miss Sterling ain't cork-brained!"

"Thank you for your kind words, Mr. Sneed," responded Ivy, who had entered the saloon unnoticed, since all eyes were upon Westbrook. "And I do apologize for causing such a problem for everyone."

Sneed looked properly self-conscious, and Randall Montgomery responded quickly, "Nonsense, Miss Sterling. You caused no problem, and why you left is none of our affair. We are only grateful you are home safely."

There was a murmur of agreement, and Ivy smiled at him for rescuing her. She had not the slightest intention of explaining to them why she had left, certain they would all know it soon enough. Doubtless Edmund and Miss Evans had held their tongues for fear she was lost and they would be indirectly responsible for her death. Now that she was safe, Miss Evans would be free to tell the others about her conquest of Edmund Montgomery. Ivy straightened her shoulders. Miss Evans would soon discover which of them Edmund cared for.

"Now it is time to begin rehearsal!" announced Mr. Ravensby suddenly, having once more heaped his plate with sausages and feeling restored. "We have lost a full day, and now we must make the most of our time! Miss Sterling, we will need you and Mr. Edmund Montgomery on stage for the parting of the lovers."

Self-consciously, the two of them presented themselves to Mr. Ravensby and Miss Durrell, prepared to be moved about and instructed to within an inch of their lives. Fortunately, Ivy thought gratefully, they were kept so occupied that there was no opportunity for any awkwardness between them. All too soon, young Romeo was on his way to Mantua, and Juliet was left to face Miss Evans, who was playing her mother, Lady Capulet. Ivy was delighted to be able to vent all of her anger in that scene, denouncing her parents' intention to marry her to Paris with such fervor that Mr. Ravensby was moved to applaud her at the close of the scene.

There was a brief break for refreshments, during which Ivy and Edmund sought a secluded corner to talk in whispers.

"Dearest lady, I wanted to explain to you about that night in the bookroom," Edmund began earnestly, taking her hand and leaning close to her.

"I told you there was no need to explain, Edmund," she returned softly. "It was not your fault at all."

The young man looked puzzled, and she nodded her head reassuringly. "Truly it was not. Mr. Westbrook wrote you the note that said to meet me there."

He looked still more puzzled. "Mr. Westbrook wrote me a note? Why would he write me a note pretending to be you?"

"Jealousy," she said briefly. "He also sent a note to Miss Evans, telling her to meet you there and to bring a lock of her hair, and he also left a note for me so I would arrive in time to find the two of you together."

Prudently, Mr. Montgomery did not remind her he had been embracing Miss Evans. Instead, he focused his attention on Mr. Westbrook. "But why would he do such a very strange thing?" he asked. "What did you mean when you said jealousy was his reason?"

Before she could answer, his eyebrows drew close together and he asked sharply, "Do you mean he has formed an attachment for you?"

Pleased by this sign of possessiveness on her lover's part, Ivy did not deny it, trying to decide whether or not she should mention the kisses.

"Tell me about the night you spent together in the gatehouse!" Mr. Montgomery demanded, his voice growing louder.

She saw to her dismay that the others had heard him, and all of them were looking at the young couple. Then, just as quickly, eyes turned toward Mr. Westbrook.

"Yes, do tell all of us," said Miss Evans, delighted by this turn of events. "I have been wondering just what happened out there in the gatehouse."

Ivy colored and Westbrook's expression darkened ominously. "If you mean to imply, Miss Evans, that there was some impropriety, then I think you should apologize to your hostess. That remark was both tasteless and unnecessary."

Miss Evans shrugged. "I was not the only one wondering. You heard Mr. Montgomery ask it first. Was his remark also tasteless and unnecessary?"

"Indeed it was!" snapped Westbrook. "It was not the remark of a gentleman!"

Edmund Montgomery sat straighter, and a pleasurable ripple of excitement ran through the group. Dramatic moments were welcome, both on and off the stage.

"Are you saying, Westbrook, that I am not a gentleman?" he demanded.

"How great a slow-top are you, Montgomery?" asked Westbrook in disgust. "I believe that is exactly what I said. And I would like to call to your attention that your concern is all for yourself instead of the injury being done to the young lady's reputation."

"I am perfectly capable of defending Miss Sterling's reputation!" retorted Montgomery.

"By bandying about such a question as you asked in a group such as this?" asked Westbrook, his brows high in disbelief. "I do not know which you are, sir—a clodpole or a cad—but in neither case should you be speaking about a young lady such as Miss Sterling, who is far your superior in intelligence and breeding!"

"That is unforgivable!" shouted Montgomery, ignoring Ivy's restraining hand on his arm and leaping to his feet. "I demand satisfaction, sir!"

"And I shall be pleased to oblige you," returned Westbrook, unmoved, "although I usually only duel with gentlemen."

"Please, Edmund, Mr. Westbrook," said Randall Montgomery, who had entered the room for the last part of the exchange. "Pray remember you are guests in someone else's home and your nerves are on edge because of being confined by the storm. Do not act in haste."

At this point, Mr. Ravensby, who had adjourned

to his own chamber to put on his costume, returned, ready to proceed with the rehearsal.

"Places, everyone!" he called as he entered the saloon, blissfully unaware of the dramatic scene he was interrupting. "If we stay on schedule, we shall finish the run-through before supper and have time to go back to practice some scenes tonight. I daresay we shall be ready to present it tomorrow."

Miss Durrell and Alistair Sterling entered close on his heels, and the rehearsal began promptly. With great intensity, Ravensby, now engulfed by a large dark dressing gown to represent Friar Laurence's habit, counseled the distraught Juliet to take the potion he had prepared for her. With equal intensity, Juliet swore she would. Before supper arrived, Juliet had been carried to her tomb and Romeo had found her there, taking his own life for love of her.

"And so would I willingly die for you, dear Ivy," he whispered to her after she had awakened to find her Romeo dead, and plunged a theatrical dagger between her arm and her body, falling gracefully over her lover. "Like Romeo, I do not wish to live without my Juliet."

"Really now, do remember you are dead!" snapped Ravensby irritably. "It is most unprofessional to have bodies whispering to one another on the stage when they are supposed to be dead. Think of your audience!"

Obediently, the bodies subsided to silence, and Edmund satisfied himself with pressing his lips inconspicuously to Ivy's fingers.

The grieving parents were brought onstage to view the fruits of their quarrel, and Alistair Sterling, as the Prince, gravely pointed out to them that there had never been "a story of more woe, Than this of Juliet and her Romeo."

"Bravo!" called Ravensby, still swathed in the dressing gown. "We have made it in good time. Wonderful work, everyone! We shall return to rehearsal as soon as we fortify ourselves with supper."

The company ate with enthusiasm, perhaps because they felt that death had come so close to them with the storm, or because they had completed the play, or because they hoped for a renewal of hostilities between Westbrook and Edmund Montgomery.

"I trust this storm will soon come to an end," ventured Miss Floyd, eager to introduce a topic of conversation that could cause no controversy.

"Sam McGrundy says it is showing signs of moving on," said Mr. Westbrook, who had earlier journeyed once more to the stable. "Soon we will be able to travel again."

His announcement was greeted with a buzz of general conversation and a variety of reactions within the hearts of his listeners. Mr. Sterling, realizing Miss Durrell would soon be slipping away from him, gazed at her longingly, although the lady appeared unaware of his attention as she chatted with Miss Floyd. Ivy and Edmund Montgomery gazed deeply into one another's eyes, while Westbrook and Randall Montgomery watched them uneasily. Miss Evans heaved a sigh of relief, eager to be removed from a place where she had no admirer, and Sneed and Jarvis talked eagerly of the dinners and Mrs. Rollins of the card games that awaited them at the estate of the Earl of Lakeside.

"How will you manage when we all leave you, Miss Sterling?" asked Westbrook, determined to interrupt the lovers. "Surely Foxridge Hall will seem peaceful once again after we have gone."

His ploy did not work. Ivy did not even look up at him. Instead her gaze remained fixed on Edmund.

"I don't know how I shall manage when you are gone," she said, looking into Montgomery's eyes. "I will be unbearably lonely. I cannot imagine Foxridge Hall without you."

Westbrook glanced at Randall Montgomery and raised his eyebrows. "You will have to do it," he murmured.

Montgomery sighed and nodded. "I don't wish to, but I agree. There is nothing else to be done."

Mr. Ravensby, having finished his supper, repaired to the stage and clapped his hands.

"All right, everyone! Let's begin at the beginning and take it straight through. Places, everyone!"

The rehearsal progressed smoothly, with Mr. Ravensby reminding them at frequent intervals that they would be performing for a real audience the next day. Mr. Sterling had given permission for his servants to leave their work and have the elevating experience of viewing a play by the Bard. Mrs. McGrundy was showing signs of refusing the opportunity, but most of the others planned to attend.

The fight between Romeo and Tybalt that evening was conducted with rapiers, and both of the gentlemen proved themselves to be expert swordsmen. However, when Tybalt collapsed upon Mr. Ravensby's cue, supposedly having sustained a mortal wound, Edmund Montgomery proved to be a particularly vengeful Romeo. Instead of staring down at the body of his slain foe and then fleeing as he realized what he had done, Romeo raised his rapier once more, apparently planning to pierce Tybalt one last time. Before Ravensby could interfere, Westbrook, seeing what was coming, grabbed his own weapon and knocked the rapier from Edmund Montgomery's hand.

"Coward!" he exclaimed. "That is precisely what I would have expected of you, Montgomery!"

Miss Durrell and Ravensby, realizing that the two players appeared bent upon making the scene more realistic than necessary, hurried to intercede.

"Come now, gentlemen!" Ravensby admonished them. "I believe we should go through that once more. Tybalt is not supposed to rise from the dead to continue the fight, and Romeo should not be attempting to skewer the body of the fallen Tybalt once he is dead. It is bad form."

"I must disagree with you, Reginald," said Miss Durrell, studying the expressions of Westbrook and Edmund Montgomery. "I am afraid if we repeat the scene, we might have real bodies strewing the stage."

She gently removed the rapier from Edmund's grip and turned to Westbrook. "Come now, sir," she chided in a low voice. "You are a man of the world. You know this is not suitable behavior."

He glanced at her briefly and inclined his head, then turned and walked out of the room.

Sterling had hurriedly sent Gerald to produce the bowl of punch, deciding they needed something to break the tension. And, as it usually did, the punch caused everyone to relax, although Westbrook did not return to the saloon and Edmund Montgomery continued to mutter darkly about those who took too much upon themselves and interfered in the business of others.

"A real gentleman would answer my challenge," he told Ivy as he drank a second cup of punch. "Westbrook is afraid to meet me."

Ivy, who was less convinced of Westbrook's timidity, was still not eager to have Edmund face a man she considered a formidable adversary.

"It is just because he is unhappy, Edmund," she whispered, thinking of what Miss Durrell had said about her uncle. "There is no need to mind him."

She did not add she hoped there would be no repeat performance of his attempt to strike Westbrook while he was down. That had shocked her somewhat, but she ascribed it to the tension. In the meantime, as she looked into his eyes, she was willing to believe anything he might tell her.

Sitting quietly by the fire, Randall Montgomery watched it all and shook his head. Westbrook had been correct. Little though he wished to do it, he would be forced to speak with Miss Sterling about his brother.

Seventeen

As Alistair Sterling and all of his guests once again reluctantly gathered their candles and prepared for the long, icy trek to their chambers, Westbrook mentioned to Mr. Ravensby that Edmund Montgomery had indicated an interest in assistance with his role as Romeo and had asked that they spend a little time together going over his questions after the others had gone up to bed. Delighted by this display of interest in perfecting his performance, Ravensby bore down upon Montgomery and cut him out neatly from the others, successfully separating him from Miss Sterling.

Having done his work, Westbrook caught Randall Montgomery's eye and nodded. Prepared to do his duty, little though he liked it, that gentleman made his way to Ivy's side and bowed.

"Miss Sterling, I was wondering if you might give me a little of your time before you retire for the evening," he said in a low voice.

Ivy looked at him with surprise. Edmund's brother was, she knew, a very quiet, reticent sort of gentleman, and she had exchanged no more than five minutes of conversation with him during their stay at the Hall.

"Of course," she agreed. "Shall we talk here?"

He glanced about the room. Most of the others were already on their way up the stairs, while Ravensby had Edmund cornered on the stage, walking him step by step through the fight scenes once more. Since Westbrook had managed to slip away, Ravensby had also appropriated Jarvis and Sneed to stand in for Tybalt and Benvolio, while he himself played Mercutio. He had relinquished the role to Miss Durrell with great reluctance, although the lady was known for her breeches roles and her dexterity with a sword. This would give him an opportunity to show them what the scene should look like with a proper Mercutio. A glance at Ravensby was enough to inform Randall Montgomery that they would be occupying the saloon for the next hour or two.

"Is there a place more private?" he asked Ivy. "My business is quite personal, and it pertains to my brother."

Her interest truly piqued now, Ivy nodded. "Of course. We may use my uncle's bookroom. He has already gone to bed, and the fire in the bookroom will make it habitable."

Quietly they made their way there, accompanied by MacTavish, and Ivy closed the door firmly behind her, trying not to remember her last unhappy experience in this room. After they were seated close to the fire, she looked at her guest in some concern, for even in the firelight, his face looked drawn and weary.

"What is it, Mr. Montgomery?" she asked. "Are you unwell? Is there something wrong?"

He nodded, setting down the books he had been carrying upon the floor beside his chair. Or she had thought they were books. One, she saw, was a small chest, which he placed upon his lap.

"It grieves me to tell you something that must give you pain, Miss Sterling, but I feel I must do so."

Ivy could feel a cold hand clutching at her heart, but she did not allow herself to betray any emotion. The man before her looked distraught enough for both of them. Comforted by her dog's warm presence against her foot, she leaned down and stroked the terrier's head.

"What is it, Mr. Montgomery?" she asked gently, trying to help him. "You said it was about your brother?"

He nodded, not meeting her eyes. Finally, he straightened his shoulders and forced himself to look at her directly.

"Please understand, Miss Sterling, that I would not be telling you my brother's private affairs if I felt I had any other choice. However, I cannot allow you to be hurt by Edmund any more than you already have been."

There was another lengthy pause while Ivy waited and he struggled to find the words. So, she thought bleakly, Mr. Westbrook had told her the truth after all. She had thought perhaps he had fabricated the information in an attempt to warn her away from a man he considered unsuitable, but a glance at Randall Montgomery's face told her the truth.

"Edmund has always had a great need for excitement in his life," began Mr. Montgomery. "I say this not as an excuse, but as an explanation. He has been so from the time he was a boy. He was a neck-or-nothing rider, never bothered by spills or broken limbs, and so he still is."

Ivy nodded encouragingly. This was not so very terrible, after all. She knew Edmund was adventurous, and she found it a very appealing quality. Perhaps that was what his quiet brother found so distressing.

"Yes, I have recognized that in him, Mr. Montgomery. That is true of many young men his age, I believe."

"It is something more with Edmund," he said. "When there is no excitement available, I am afraid he creates it."

Ivy repressed a smile at this admission, because she could see Randall felt that he was imparting terrible news to her. Clearly, he had had little experience with high-spirited young men. Ivy had seen enough when spending time with her parents' friends and their children to know the need to create excitement was not peculiar to Edmund Montgomery. She had heard of the young men's races and the Four-in-Hand Club and the infamous betting books at the gentlemen's clubs. Mr. Montgomery, as a cleric, must have led a very sheltered life, she reflected.

"That too is common to other young gentlemen, Mr. Montgomery. Perhaps you are too hard upon your brother."

He shook his head. "I mean when he creates his excitement, he does so with no notion of right or wrong, forgetting what is honorable or dishonorable."

Ivy had no reply for this, nor could she imagine just what he meant by the comment, so she waited patiently until he could continue.

"I know I must be more particular in order for you to understand, Miss Sterling, but it grieves me to do so." After another pause, he forced himself to go on. "For instance, when he was seventeen, he became a highwayman."

"A highwayman!" she exclaimed, jolted by this unexpected news. "Do you mean he actually held up coaches?"

Mr. Montgomery nodded. "At least four before my father and I discovered it. We were able to recover most of the money and jewels and return them to their appropriate owners without revealing who had taken them."

"Well," faltered Ivy, "that is very bad, to be sure, but again, he was just a boy then." She did not bother to add he had been her very age when he had done those things.

"He also gambles, Miss Sterling—far too much, I am afraid."

"Well, certainly that is a failing of many young gentlemen—and older ones as well," she returned, thinking of the stories she had heard from her mother and father. Gambling, in fact, seemed to be both one of the most favored amusements and most dangerous pastimes of their society. She did not like to think of Edmund gambling, to be sure, but there were worse things.

"He also signed my father's name on the deed of sale for several pieces of land," Mr. Montgomery went on, determined now to lay it all out for her. He could see she would not easily believe his brother was not to be trusted. "He needed money to pay his gambling debts, and so he sold off land that had belonged to our family for generations The new owners turned the tenants off their farms and left them homeless. My father was, literally, heartbroken by this betrayal, and he died soon thereafter."

A long silence fell as Ivy stared into the fire, trying to take in this information and reconcile it with the picture of Edmund she had painted for herself.

"I am so very sorry, Mr. Montgomery—about your father and for you and what you must have suffered," she said in a voice barely above a whisper.

"And I appreciate that, Miss Sterling, but surely you can see what I mean about Edmund. He is a very charming, very appealing person, and I love him because he is my brother—but he also appears to be entirely without a conscience. I can never make him see that anything he has done is wrong. That is why I have made arrangements to take him as far away from proper society as possible, to a place where his adventurous nature will work to his advantage. If we settle in North America after the war, we will go to the frontier, where there are few laws and Edmund may have a better chance."

Another long silence ensued, and finally Ivy

looked at him. "You are a very devoted brother, Mr. Montgomery," she said sincerely. "Edmund is fortunate to have you looking after him."

"He is my responsibility," Randall Montgomery replied simply. "That is why I felt I had to tell you the truth about him. I do not wish for him to cause needless harm, and I hoped to prevent further pain to you, Miss Sterling."

She nodded. "And I appreciate your frankness, sir. But had you considered that perhaps I might help you care for him? I do not know if he has told you, but Edmund has declared his love for me, and we have spoken of marriage. Perhaps that might offer him the stability that he needs."

Mr. Montgomery sighed. "I am afraid you have been misled, Miss Sterling," he said gently. "You see, you are not the first lady he has proposed to, nor will you be the last. The difficulty is that he does not mean what he says, and he has no conscience in his dealings with women either."

"His dealings with women?" she whispered, her lips scarcely forming the words. "Do you mean that there have been a great many others?"

Mr. Montgomery nodded grimly, his lips thin. "He has eloped several times, but he has always been stopped by me or the family of the lady, and his liaisons with ladies he has no intention of marrying have been many. As for young women like yourself, let me show you."

Here he reluctantly opened the wooden box he had been carrying with his books. In it lay a shining mass of curls —curls of all colors, from midnight black to pale silver to glowing red, some bound with ribbons, some lying free. Ivy could see there were too many to count at a glance, and she recognized her own and that of Miss Evans.

"Edmund says that he collects these curls as the Indians in North America do scalps—only instead of showing his prowess in battle, they show how proficient a lover he is."

He did not look at her for a moment or two, because he knew he had delivered the final blow. The young lady might be willing to sacrifice herself in order to help the man she loved and who loved her in return, but he knew Miss Sterling was far too intelligent a young woman to throw herself away on a man with the attitude he had just described.

When he finally looked up, she was regarding him somberly. "Thank you, Mr. Montgomery," she said. "I know it was difficult for you to tell me these things and that you did it only out of concern for me."

He nodded, closing the chest and gathering up his books. As he rose to leave, he patted her shoulder briefly. "I know this is painful," he said gently, "but it is far better you suffer now instead of making a serious error and living with the pain for a lifetime."

She nodded silently, patting MacTavish and staring into the fire.

"May I light your way up the stairs?" he asked, hating to leave her alone after she had received such distressing news.

Ivy shook her head and managed to smile up at him. "Thank you, but no, Mr. Montgomery. And you need not fear," she added, seeing his troubled expression. "I shall not go running out into the storm because of this."

Somewhat reassured, he bowed and slowly made his way down the passageway to the stairs. As he passed the yellow saloon, he could hear Ravensby's voice and knew the victims were still engaged in rehearsing the fight scene. Their voices and the clang of metal against metal punctuated the stillness of the Hall.

Ivy had been sitting alone for some minutes when she heard the door open. She looked up, prepared to see Mr. Montgomery again, back to add one more morsel of horrifying information to the case against Edmund. To her astonishment and annoyance, however, Mr. Westbrook was the caller.

"There is no need for you to come here, sir," she said, looking away from him. "Mr. Montgomery has already informed me of his brother's past, and I have assured him the news will not send me running into the night once more."

"I am relieved to hear that, of course," returned Westbrook, seating himself in Montgomery's chair without asking leave. "I have no strength to make that trip through the snow again. However, I could stand no longer in the passageway, either. I am certain I was developing chilblains in that damnable icy draft."

Here he rose and stood for a moment with his back to the fire, holding his hands out, palm first, behind him.

"Standing in the passageway?" echoed Ivy, startled. "Why should you be standing out there in the dark and the cold?"

Westbrook shrugged. "You have just said it yourself. It occurred to me also that you might choose to run away rather than face the truth about Edmund Montgomery. I wanted to be present to stop you before you reached the damned door."

Ivy was torn between annoyance that he was once again interfering and gratitude that he should be willing to place himself at considerable inconvenience for her sake.

"You are all kindness," she replied, the decided edge to her voice giving the lie to her words.

He did not reply, and after a silence long enough to make her uncomfortable, she looked up at him. He was, as she had been certain he was, studying her. She flushed but said nothing, determined not to be the one to break the silence.

"I must congratulate you," he said finally. "I was afraid I would come in to find you in a puddle of tears or to see you had given way to the vapors or hysteria. I am pleased to see you are managing so calmly."

"I don't know what business it is of yours to congratulate me or to criticize me for my behavior, Mr. Westbrook!" she snapped. "Indeed, I fail to see why you have inserted yourself in my affairs at all!"

She was more than a little angry with him, but she was none too pleased with herself after that speech, either. Although she knew she was justified in being angry with him for his interfering ways, he had, after all, risked his own life when he had thought her lost in the storm. Her irritation grew. She did not wish to feel any obligation to this annoying man.

Westbrook, meanwhile, was watching her with interest. "You are still quite transparent, Miss Sterling," he observed. "You are doing much better at controlling yourself, but you need to show the internal struggle less."

"Oh, do be quiet, sir!" she snapped.

To her profound annoyance, he was. A silence descended that threatened to last the night—or until one of them departed. The only sound was the terrier's gentle snoring. His chin was on Ivy's foot, but she noticed with irritation he had stretched himself in such a manner that one of his hind legs lay next to Westbrook's boot. This mark of familiar acceptance on the part of her dog was further aggravation. She preferred MacTavish snap at the man's boots rather than lie comfortably next to them.

The minutes ticked by, and Ivy finally broke. "Why are you still here, Mr. Westbrook?" she demanded. "Is your only wish to gloat over my unhappiness?"

"Do you hear me gloating?" he asked reasonably.

"No, but you could be gloating just by standing there and watching me. What other reason could you have for staying?"

"To be certain you are all right," he responded simply.

"But I have assured you I will not run away again!" she exclaimed impatiently.

"Saying that does not mean you are all right, however," he observed. "The very fact you are still sitting here indicates a troubled mind."

"Well, naturally I am troubled! I assume you know very well what Mr. Randall Montgomery has just told me about his brother."

He nodded. "And we were both sorry you had to hear those things, Miss Sterling. But you deserved to know them."

"It must gratify you to know you were correct," she remarked bitterly, "and that I am indeed as hen-witted as all the countless young women who have thrown themselves at Edmund."

"I am not at all gratified," he returned. "Nor do I think you are hen-witted, as I tried to point out to you when we were at the gatehouse. I think very highly of your intelligence, and I did not think you deserved to be misled."

"I was not misled!" she said, her tone tart. "Edmund did not mislead me. Or at least," she added, wishing to be strictly truthful, "for the most part he did not mislead me. I believe I must have made up my own picture of Edmund Montgomery."

"Now that," he said, moving abruptly toward her and disturbing MacTavish, who rolled over indignantly, "is the type of remark I would expect from you, Miss Sterling! Have you thought about what part of the picture was really Edmund Montgomery and how much of it was your own doing?" He sat down again and pulled his chair close to hers.

Ivy nodded reluctantly. She needed to talk to someone, and she supposed he would do as well as any. There was certainly no one else she could turn to.

"I did not need to make up the fact that he is

charming or handsome," she said slowly, "nor that he is daring."

"No," Westbrook conceded. "Although I cannot see the charm myself, I recognize many feel he possesses it. And certainly he is a well-set-up young man and daring enough to be eager to go to war."

"Well," Ivy continued, more reluctantly still, "it may be everything else I added myself."

"And what other qualities did you give him that he does not possess, Miss Sterling?"

For a moment she forgot her annoyance with Westbrook, and she was grateful just to be able to think through her trouble aloud. There was almost a comfort in his presence, for at least she was not speaking to the empty air, nor to Mac-Tavish, who could do no more than whine or growl his comments.

"I suppose I believed him to be sincere," she mused, "an honest, frank man—though I discovered, of course, he merely told me what he thought I wished to hear."

"And so you prize sincerity, ma'am?" he asked.

"Well, of course I do, Mr. Westbrook!" she responded indignantly. "Just what sort of a frippery miss do you think I am?"

"I do not think you a frippery miss at all," he replied, smiling. "Do continue. What other qualities did you bestow upon Mr. Montgomery?"

"Loyalty to those he cares for," she said unwillingly. "That is something he certainly did not show to me, but then he did not truly care for me, so that is not a fair test. However, he did not show any loyalty to his own father, and the consequences of that were unthinkable."

Westbrook nodded thoughtfully. "What else?"

"Although I hate to say it, intelligence," Ivy said. "For all I am not needle-witted, I had to admit when you called him a slow-top for not following what you were saying to him in the saloon, I quite agreed with you. He is often so self-absorbed that he cannot think clearly about other matters."

It pained her to say that aloud, particularly to Mr. Westbrook, but she knew it to be true. Whatever imperfections she might have, Ivy did not allow herself to lie—to herself or to others.

Again Westbrook nodded with satisfaction. "You are a remarkable young woman, Miss Sterling. The qualities you prized in your young man—the qualities you discovered that he does not possess—speak very well for the kind of person you are."

"I am overcome by your approval," she said dryly. "I only wish I could have come by it in an easier manner."

To her surprise, Westbrook, who had pulled his chair around to face her, took both her hands in his and pulled her closer to him, so their faces were very near.

"I grant you, Miss Sterling, I am not a handsome man nor a charming one, nor am I daring enough to wish to go away to war, but the other characteristics you named I believe I do possess."

Thrown completely off guard by his unexpected behavior, Ivy thought frantically for a response. With relief, she seized upon one.

"Loyalty to those you care for?" she asked, raising her brows. "I believe, sir, you told me you do not trouble yourself about others."

"Loyalty to those I care for?" he repeated, inching closer. "That would be to you, Miss Sterling, for I am very much afraid I do care for you." Here he pulled her to him and kissed her soundly.

When Ivy emerged breathless from his embrace, she caught the lapels of his coat and looked into his eyes. "I thought you said I am a schoolroom miss, too young to be in company with others," she reminded him. "Your behavior smacks of the hypocrite, Mr. Westbrook!"

"I have changed my mind," he said simply, kissing her once more.

Abruptly he stood up, pulling her to her feet and pointing her toward the door.

"And now that you have reminded me of my responsibility to you, ma'am, I believe we must take ourselves away. If we are very quick and very quiet, we may make it past Mr. Ravensby and company in the yellow saloon."

Gathering MacTavish under her arm so he would make no noise, Ivy and Westbrook stole quietly past the saloon to the stairway, Mr. Westbrook lighting their way.

"Parry, Jarvis, parry!" they heard Mr. Ravensby yell impatiently as they stole past the door. "You will be run through if you insist upon standing there after every thrust!"

They could not hear Jarvis's reply, but fled

silently up the stairs before anyone could emerge from the saloon.

Once back in her chamber, Ivy placed MacTavish in his basket by the fire and patted his head.

"Well, Mac, it has been a very long day. I have lost a lover I wanted and won one I don't wish to have."

As she lay sleepless in bed, considering the events of the day, Ivy found it difficult to overcome her longing for Edmund. His manner had been so gracious, so loverlike, that she would not have credited his insincerity if she had heard of it from anyone save his brother. It was strange she could not cry over it, though.

Stranger still, she thought, was Mr. Westbrook's sudden declaration of affection. No doubt he meant well enough, and his kisses, both at the gatehouse and tonight in the bookroom, had been pleasing, even exciting. She had discovered, to her surprise, that she rather liked him—and she admitted to herself he had indeed gone to considerable trouble on her behalf. Nonetheless, she was quite certain she did not love him as she had loved Edmund.

Tomorrow would be a difficult day, she knew, for she would have to play Juliet to Edmund's Romeo, knowing all the while she no longer cared for him and that he had never cared for her. She would be playing the love scenes with a stranger.

Eighteen

Early the next morning, Ivy and MacTavish made their way to the kitchen, Ivy eager for cheerful company and MacTavish for breakfast before the fire.

"Good morning, Mrs. McGrundy," she said brightly as she entered. As usual, the kitchen smelled of baking bread and cinnamon, freshly ground coffee beans and sizzling sausages. Even had she not been hungry, Ivy would have been content just to breathe in the fragrances of the room.

"Good morning, Miss Sterling," replied Mrs. McGrundy. "We are up to twelve now, miss. I told you how it would be."

"Twelve silver spoons?" inquired Ivy. That was, she thought, getting to be quite a few. She had not really been surprised one or two might have been slipped into pockets or reticules, but twelve silver spoons was a substantial loss.

"Have you mentioned the matter to my uncle?" she inquired.

"I tried to do so, miss, when he came to tell us about attending the play," she said darkly, "but it was clear he didn't listen to a word I had to say."

"Well, we shall have to see what we can find out about this," said Ivy. At least Edmund probably hadn't pilfered the spoons. He appeared to save himself for larger robberies.

She let MacTavish out and then quickly back in again. "Why, it's snowing again," she said, astonished. "I thought that the snow had let up yesterday afternoon."

"And so it did," Mrs. McGrundy assured her, "but the wind has risen again and the snow started about the time Betty came down to stoke the fire before dawn broke."

The little maid nodded. "Mr. Westbrook was using his rope to get to the stables again this morning," she observed, "so I knew it was still bad out."

"Sam and his stablehands will be using it when they come in to watch the play," observed Mrs. McGrundy, carefully preparing a pot of chocolate for Ivy and a mug of cider for Mr. Westbrook when he should return.

"I'm very glad they are taking the time to come to the play," said Ivy brightly, trying to be happy about performing the play, although she was dreading seeing Edmund once more. "Will you be coming, too, Mrs. McGrundy?"

The cook shook her head. "Even if I wanted to see such a thing—and I don't—I need to be here to fix the supper and to fix the refreshments the master wants brought in for the play."

"I offered to stay, miss," said Betty, "but she won't hear of it."

"You want to go and see young spindle-shanks.

He's been hanging about here every chance he gets, and at least he seems better than the rest of that lot. And, at any rate, I need to stay here to keep an eye on the pantry to be certain no one takes every piece of silver the master owns."

"I do wish you would come, Mrs. McGrundy," Ivy coaxed her. "You would get to see me perform."

"Yes, miss, I know I would," she replied grimly. "And forgive me for saying so, since it isn't my place to do so, but you shouldn't be standing up in front of the servants with that pack of playactors. It isn't seemly."

"Well," Ivy sighed, as she and MacTavish settled in front of the fire for breakfast, "I still wish you would come. I think you'd be surprised at how much you would enjoy it."

"I hear there's sword fighting in the play, miss," the cook observed. "Does Mr. Sneak get run through?"

"There is swordplay, but Mr. Sneed is not killed during any of the fights," Ivy replied, smiling at the question.

Mrs. McGrundy snorted. "If you had told me he was, I might have seen the purpose of plays—having something happen to people on the stage that ought to happen to them in real life. I might even have come to see it."

Ivy drank her cup of chocolate quickly and left the kitchen sooner than she might have. Knowing Mr. Westbrook was in the stable and might appear at any moment lent her speed. She had no desire to see that gentleman any more quickly than necessary this morning. She did not even know how she should look at him now that he had kissed her and told her he cared for her.

When he had kissed her that morning in the gatehouse, she had thought he was weary and still half asleep. He probably had thought her someone else until he had awakened fully. Last night, however, he had known quite certainly who she was.

She and MacTavish hurried down the passageways to the yellow saloon. The wind was indeed rising; she could hear its whistling and the icy grains of snow being thrown against the windows, and the drafts were enough to make her wish she had worn a pelisse instead of a shawl.

She was not surprised to see that the saloon was alive with activity when she entered. Mr. Ravensby was in his element, ordering people about and delivering his pre-performance advice freely. He had apparently just reduced little Miss Floyd to tears, and Mrs. Rollins was in the process of informing him that offering further advice could be detrimental to his health.

When Edmund looked up and saw her, she realized uncomfortably he had put down his sword and the cloak he would wear and was hurrying toward her. She had dreaded this moment.

"Dearest Ivy," he murmured, taking her hand before she could stop him, "as you saw last night, Mr. Ravensby stopped me before I could escape, and we spent hours rehearsing. I would have greatly preferred to spend the time with you."

Ivy managed to disengage her hand. "That is quite all right, Mr. Montgomery," she replied pleasantly. "I believe it is just as well you were busy."

"Why?" he demanded, trying to recapture her hand and attempting to meet her eyes, which she resolutely kept him from doing. "Why would you not wish to be with me?"

"Perhaps because she prefers the company of gentlemen," observed Mr. Westbrook pleasantly. He had strolled into the room and approached the pair, who had been too deeply absorbed in their own little drama to notice him.

Montgomery glared at him. "By gad, sir, you have made a habit of insulting me! I will have my satisfaction today, whether I am a guest in Foxridge Hall or not! I will not tolerate such treatment!"

Westbrook shrugged. "As you wish," he said. "Just keep your distance from Miss Sterling."

"And how do you propose I do that?" he demanded. "I am playing Romeo to her Juliet, if you recall, sir!"

"I recall," said Westbrook over his shoulder, for he was moving toward the fire. "But off the stage you will keep your distance, sir."

"Do you wish me to keep my distance?" Edmund asked, turning back to Ivy.

She looked at him a moment, admiring the depth of his blue eyes and the earnestness of his expression. Then she nodded. "I believe it would be best, Mr. Montgomery," she replied.

"But why, Miss Sterling?" he demanded. "You

must give me some reason for the change in your affections."

Thinking of her conversation with Mr. Westbrook the night before, Ivy shook her head. "I believe there was no real affection, sir. I think I made up a story about who you were—and certainly you feel no true affection for me."

"How can you say that?" he cried. "How can you be so cold? Of course I care for you deeply!"

"And that is why you embraced Miss Evans and took one of her yellow curls?"

"Ah, so it is jealousy!" he exclaimed, his eyes brightening. "But you know that was a mistake! You told me so yourself! You said Westbrook had tricked us all by sending us the notes! Why turn on me when it is his fault?"

Some of the others, who had been listening with interest, looked at each other with lifted brows.

"Mr. Westbrook sent me that note?" asked Rosa Evans, interrupting abruptly. "You did not write to me, Mr. Montgomery?"

Edmund shook his head impatiently. "Of course not! He asked you to meet me and to bring a lock of your hair."

"But you accepted it, sir, and you kissed me, if you recall. Did he tell you to do that, too?"

Edmund flushed as a ripple of laughter ran round the group. "Of course not! That simply happened—and it meant nothing!"

"So it did!" she replied sharply, looking at him as she might a bug she had squashed underfoot. "At least we agree upon that much!"

It was beginning to look as though the drama would be taking place offstage, so Mr. Ravensby came over to hustle the others into action.

"Breakfast will arrive at any moment, and we must eat quickly and then make our final preparations," he informed them.

"I don't know as I shall eat beforehand," observed Mr. Jarvis. "Sometimes it just don't agree with me to do so."

"Then by all means, Mr. Jarvis, do not eat," urged Miss Durrell, who had entered the room with Alistair Sterling just in time to hear this remark.

She looked, thought Ivy, remarkably well in the doeskin breeches she was wearing for the role of Mercutio. And she could indeed handle a foil very handily. She glanced at her uncle and saw he looked as lovelorn as he had since Miss Durrell's arrival. She still did not care much for her uncle, but she knew he would be in a pitiable state when the troupe left, and she found herself feeling sorry for him.

Breakfast appeared, and everyone served his or her plate and adjourned to a comfortable place to dine. True to her promise to Mrs. McGrundy, Ivy kept her eyes open, but she still had not the least notion of who was responsible for the mysterious disappearance of the silver spoons. Mr. Ravensby, she noticed, was once again enjoying a plate heaped with sausages, and Mr. Jarvis appeared to have decided he could force down a morsel or two. The red woolen scarf he had lent to Westbrook as a marker during the trip to the gatehouse had tinally dried and was once again wrapped gaily around his neck to ward off the drafts.

To her surprise, Miss Durrell beckoned to her, and Ivy dutifully hurried over. The lady's charm remained as strong as ever, and Ivy felt a faint glow when Miss Durrell turned her smile and the full warmth of her gaze upon her.

"You look wonderful, my dear—glowing the way Juliet should as she thinks of her Romeo."

Ivy was not certain that she had been glowing, but she felt any glow would have assuredly slipped away at this reminder of her Romeo.

Unaware of the change in Ivy's affections, Miss Durrell continued, "I have been speaking with your uncle about you, Miss Sterling, and he would like to have a private word with you before the play begins. He has something to show you and something to tell you as well."

Mystified, Ivy looked at her uncle, and he nodded. "If you could come with me now, Ivy, for just a few minutes."

Obediently, Ivy followed him from the saloon, and her heart sank as she saw she was once again retiring to the bookroom. It seemed to her she had spent altogether too much time there recently, and she wished devoutly there were another chamber with a fire where they could talk.

"Come in, my dear," said her uncle, opening the door for her and closing it behind MacTavish, who had dutifully accompanied them.

Ivy noted the "my dear" with incredulity. Her uncle had never used a term of affection with her at all. He had, in fact, almost never called her by her name.

Once again she seated herself by the fire, and once again she found herself facing a gentleman who had important news to impart. From the pocket of his jacket, he withdrew a small jeweled case and opened it, handing it to Ivy. It contained, she saw, a delicate miniature of her mother. This was the one Miss Durrell had spoken of.

"It is a lovely likeness of my mother, sir," she observed, closing the case and handing it back to him.

"I would like you to have it, Ivy," he said, returning it to her hand. "Much as I have treasured it, I would like to give it to you now."

"But, Uncle," she protested, "I do have a likeness of my parents. You need not give me yours."

"I wanted to explain to you, my dear," he said, opening the case again and looking at her mother's face, "just why I have treated you so poorly."

He looked up at her and added hurriedly, "I know this does not excuse my lack of attention to you, Ivy, but I thought that you should at least know my pitiful excuse for behaving as I have."

Although Miss Durrell had already advised her of the reason, Ivy was silent and allowed him to tell her the story of his love for her mother Gwendolyn and his bitterness when she had chosen his brother Lawrence. He had become a recluse, satisfying himself with hunting, fishing, and reading, until the recent snowstorm.

"This storm has been a godsend for me, Ivy," he

confided in her. "I have found Miss Durrell, who has promised to become my wife."

Seeing Ivy's startled expression, he nodded again, almost laughing. "Oh yes, I know it is quite unbelievable that a lady like Miss Durrell, who has so many admirers, should choose someone like me, but there it is!"

"I wish you very happy, Uncle," she murmured, meaning it. Miss Durrell as her aunt! The thought was a little difficult to take in at the moment.

"That is why I can make you a gift of the miniature of your mother, Ivy—because I am able now to go on with my own life."

Ivy nodded, accepting the miniature from his hand.

"But I wanted to tell you, too, Ivy, that as soon as Miss Durrell and I are married, you are to have your coming out in London."

Ivy looked at him in astonishment, and he laughed at her expression. She realized, still more astonished, that she had never heard him laugh before.

He nodded his head to assure her and patted her hand. "It will all happen very soon, my dear, and then you will be taken to London. Miss Durrell has made me see how wrong I have been to keep you walled up here with me. Now we shall both be set free."

"Thank you, Uncle," she replied, meaning it. Finally a trip to the bookroom had brought her good news, she thought. In fact, it was almost too much to take in at the moment. The past year had made

her so accustomed to feeling like a prisoner that
she could not believe she was about to be liberated.

Smiling, her uncle rose and offered her his arm.
"Perhaps we should return to our guests, Ivy," he
suggested. "And I would imagine the play is about
to begin."

Nineteen

And, as they entered, they saw the play was indeed about to begin. The servants were filing in to take their places on benches that had been brought in for the occasion, the breakfast dishes had been removed, and the actors were hurriedly assembling themselves behind the tapestry screens that had been arranged to serve as a makeshift curtain. Gerald and another young footman had been appointed to move them as necessary.

Ivy had time only to pause by Miss Durrell and whisper her congratulations before going to join the other actors. Edmund attempted to catch her eye, but she avoided him studiously. Mr. Jarvis was nervously moving from foot to foot, muttering that he should have left the sausages alone, for they seemed to be rising against him.

To her surprise, Ivy found she was enjoying herself. When her turn came to enter, the servants—loyal to the last one, for she had won their sympathy—stood to applaud her, and she dropped them a curtsey. The scenes with Miss Durrell as Mercutio were light and amusing, as Shakespeare had originally intended them to be, and the party scene with Edmund that she had so dreaded passed like a dream, although she was aware of a murmur of disapproval from the audience when he kissed her.

"Taking advantage of his situation, that's what!" she heard one of the maids whisper in a scandalized voice, and Ivy was glad Mrs. McGrundy was not present add her own biting commentary.

Westbrook, making his change of cloak and hat to mark his alteration from Paris to Tybalt, stopped her offstage and whispered, "Welladay, young Juliet! Even if you consider him an old man, perhaps you should reconsider the offer of marriage Paris makes to you."

She had smiled at him brightly without responding, but he had caught her arm before she could pass by him, and added, smiling down into her eyes, "I shall ask you again in truth, Miss Sterling, so think long about your answer."

Feeling as though she were walking in a dream, she moved into her next scene, climbing onto the "balcony" with the aid of Mr. Ravensby and Mr. Jarvis. The audience had relaxed and entered into the spirit of the moment, enjoying the whole affair hugely, quite as though they were on a real holiday. They called to Juliet to warn her a man was lurking in the darkness below her balcony, and they counseled Romeo loudly to be a little more forthcoming about advising the lady of his presence in her garden.

"That's a low sort of behavior, that's what it is!" exclaimed one of the stablehands. "Here he's supposed to be one of the quality, and he's acting like a curst rum touch, hanging about in the dark outside the young lady's window!"

There was a murmur of agreement, and the audience regarded Romeo with disapproval. Indeed, one of the footmen appeared ready to rise and remove Romeo forcibly from the Capulet garden and was deterred only by the sudden appearance of Mr. Ravensby and Mr. Sneed.

As the scene progressed and the servants, who were unfamiliar with the story, realized Juliet was planning to marry secretly the young man she had just met, there was a great deal of shaking of heads and muttering.

"Where's her mother then, or her governess?" asked one of the upstairs maids in an audible voice. "She's too young to be allowed to see a man alone."

When they realized the nurse was helping Juliet make the arrangements for her secret marriage, there was a ripple of outrage, and several members of the audience showed a strong desire to remind her of her duty to the young lady. Mrs. Rollins, hardened by years on the stage before difficult audiences, disregarded them and proceeded to make the wedding arrangements with Romeo.

At the close of the second act, an interval was declared so the actors could have a brief break, and selected members of the audience adjourned to the kitchen to bring the trays of refreshments prepared by Mrs. McGrundy to the saloon.

Following her master's orders, the cook had also prepared refreshments for the servants, so as soon

as they had seen to it that Mr. Sterling and his
guests were served, they all repaired to the servants'
table to enjoy themselves. Their master had always
been just with them, but he had never been a free-
handed, liberal soul, and never had he offered
them such a treat as they were enjoying. Just why he
was doing so was the subject of much speculation.

"I believe the master's top-over-tail in love," observed one of the other footmen to Gerald,
winking. "That Miss Durrell he spends his time with
has changed him, that's what!"

Several of the others nodded in agreement. Gerald, having served himself a mug of hot spiced
cider, stood and held up his cup.

"And I, for one, says God bless her!" he exclaimed. "The master is a merrier man than we
have ever seen him."

Most of the others rose and raised their cups.
"God bless her!" they echoed.

Mrs. McGrundy, who had left her kitchen for the
moment to partake of the festivities, sniffed indignantly. "An actress!" she exclaimed. "A fine kettle of
fish we will have if we gain a mistress that is one of
the playactors!"

"Come now, Sally," protested her husband, Sam.
"If Miss Durrell makes the master happy—and she
does—then what's the odds to us? Better a happy
master than one who lives in the dismals all his
born days."

The libations imbibed by the audience, along
with the general excitement of having a half holiday and a master who was in love, assured their

interest—and active participation—in the scenes that followed.

When Miss Durrell appeared in the beginning of the next act, it was all Wheeling could do to keep the audience seated and relatively silent, for they showed a marked desire to rise and cheer the lady they viewed as their new mistress. Alistair Sterling might have thought he was keeping his secrets, and certainly Ivy had been surprised by the announcement of his marriage, but the servants—as always—knew everything that was happening, often even before those most intimately involved.

So when Miss Durrell appeared, even though she was attired in doeskin breeches, a fact that had somewhat distressed the feminine portion of the audience at the beginning of the play, all of them felt kindly toward her. After all, she had caused their master to give them this unheard of liberty from work and a fine table of refreshments as their own. Also, as they had observed to Mrs. McGrundy while having refreshments, for all she was an actress, she behaved well and there appeared to be no meanness in her treatment of the household staff.

The fine bit of swordplay between Miss Durrell as Mercutio and Mr. Westbrook as Tybalt caused considerable cheering, and there was some distress when the lady fell to the floor, struck down by the vengeful Tybalt. Since they liked both of the fighters, Mr. Westbrook having made himself known among both stablehands and house servants, the audience had a difficult time deciding whom to side with. However, when the next fight was between Tybalt and Romeo, they made their choice with ease. They cheered Ty-balt unabashedly until a ragged cut appeared upon Mr. Westbrook's shoulder, and the blood began to seep through his white shirt.

"Here now! He's hurt!" exclaimed Gerald, and two or three of the audience rose as though to go to his aid.

"It's just stage blood, Gerald," one of the others assured him knowledgeably, having once attended a show in the village inn put on by a collection of traveling players.

"Well, it looks real enough to me," muttered Gerald, sinking back into his chair.

The fight, however, continued unabated, with Tybalt at last falling before Romeo. Tybalt's body was supposed to lie on stage until the end of the scene, but a quickly improvised change sent Jarvis and Sneed onstage with a litter to remove the body. Carefully they lifted Westbrook onto the litter and bore him away to the end of the room by the fire.

"You see! I told you he'd been injured!" said Jarvis to Sneed as they carried him offstage. His brow wrinkled in worry as he looked down at West-brook's shoulder. "Just look at all that blood he's already lost."

"The devil!" exclaimed Ravensby, seeing the blood. "Where is Montgomery? He removed the button from his foil, or he would never have caused you such an injury."

"I should imagine he has removed himself to safety," replied Westbrook, rising from the litter as soon as they set it down. "I don't believe he had thought about what he would do once he had managed to wound me."

"Yes, but why'd he do such a cow-hearted thing?" demanded Jarvis. "The script don't call for a real wound."

"Are you hurt badly, Westbrook?" asked Randall Montgomery, who had risen from the back of the audience and followed them, realizing the wound inflicted by his brother had been a real one. He had seen the expression on Edmund's face.

"Of course I am not," replied the victim impatiently. "It's nothing but a scratch."

"I believe I'll find young Romeo," announced Mr. Ravensby grimly. He had just calmed the audience, assuring them there was no real problem and that the play would continue as soon as possible. Now he and Jarvis rose to inspect all the corners of the room, looking behind all of the screens and the potted palms. Jarvis even drew the heavy draperies to be certain he had not secreted himself behind them. All that revealed, however, was frost-covered windows and whirling snow.

Edmund Montgomery did not seem to be still in the saloon, and the two men departed for the kitchen to bring back warm water and bandages. They did not want to draw the attention of the servants to the problem any more than was necessary.

Ivy stood in the background, watching the activity and looking at Westbrook's wound in disbelief. Even though she had learned some unpleasant truths about Edmund Montgomery, she would not have believed him capable of such a cowardly act.

To her relief, however, his victim appeared to be doing well, and when Ravensby and Jarvis reappeared, she watched Miss Durrell clean and tend Mr. Westbrook's wound.

"I'm very sorry, sir," said Miss Durrell, fixing the bandage in place. "I have no idea what made Mr. Montgomery do such a thing. You should have been quite safe in the duel."

"I will point that out to Edmund Montgomery when I have the opportunity," he replied, grinning. "I believe he did not realize that."

Ivy still stood to one side, watching during all of this. She was standing close when they removed his shirt and cleaned the wound, and she could see how unpleasant an injury he had received.

"It's quite all right, Miss Sterling," he assured her, when he looked up and saw her expression. "If the sight of blood makes you feel faint, I must tell you I agree—and I am particularly sensitive to the sight of my own blood."

"It's no laughing matter, sir," Ivy replied. "You could have been very badly injured, and it would have been my fault."

Westbrook raised his eyebrows. "You take too much upon yourself, ma'am. Why should this have been entirely your fault?"

"Because I knew I had made him angry," she said. "I should have realized that he would be particularly angry with you."

"Perhaps it was an accident," suggested Miss Floyd, who was never willing to think ill of anyone. "Certainly Mr. Montgomery would not have deliberately injured Mr. Westbrook. He is far too well bred to do such a thing."

Randall Montgomery, Ivy noted, was also gone from the saloon, doubtless in search of his brother.

As soon as the bandage was secured, Mr. Westbrook thanked Miss Durrell for her help and announced he was going to take advantage of the unexpected break and check on his horse.

"What? Go out in all this weather after you've just been injured?" exclaimed Jarvis. "You need to rest a while, sir, not go out to plunge about in the wind and snow."

"Nonsense!" Westbrook retorted. "I've done it three times a day, and I don't believe I'll have a bit more trouble going out today than I've had on other days."

He slipped his jacket over his shoulder and bowed to them briefly, then left the saloon.

"Well, one could never say he is not stubborn," observed Miss Durrell. "He is determined to do as he wishes. We can only hope he hasn't lost so much blood that he becomes weak and faints."

The rest of the group, thinking of his journey to the stable, was perturbed by this casual comment.

"I'm going to the kitchen to stop him!" announced Ivy, rising and moving to the door. "He has no business endangering himself. His horse will be quite all right. Sam is taking good care of him, and Mr. Westbrook has seen him just this morning. He must behave sensibly."

Miss Durrell laughed. "If you can make a man behave sensibly when he doesn't wish to do so, my dear, every woman in the world will demand to know your secret."

Nonetheless, Ivy and MacTavish hurried from the room. "He will have to get his greatcoat first," she remarked to her pet, "so we will wait for him in the kitchen."

Mrs. McGrundy was laboring diligently over supper, just finishing the crust on one of her inimitable meat pies. A small fleet of them stood upon the wooden table, ready to be transported to the oven.

"Well, miss, I don't wish to be the one to say I told you so, but things have come to a pretty pass when a gentleman like Mr. Westbrook is set upon in the drawing room. All because of the playactors!" she sniffed, pricking the tops of the pies with a sharp knife.

"But it wasn't because of the actors, Mrs. McGrundy," Ivy told her reluctantly. "It was Mr. Edmund Montgomery that caused the accident, I'm afraid."

"It weren't no accident. I heard the young spindle-shanks say as much when he hurried in for hot water and something to use for a bandage!"

Suddenly she stopped in the midst of pricking the crusts and looked at Ivy, her plump, rosy face suddenly looking almost pale. "You said it was one of the other gentlemen and not one of the actors, miss?"

Ivy nodded. "Mr. Edmund Montgomery," she repeated.

"Is he the young man with red hair?" the cook demanded.

Again Ivy nodded, and Mrs. McGrundy threw

down her fork and turned toward the door.
"Where's Sam?" she asked.

"Why, I should imagine he's in the saloon, waiting for the play to continue," Ivy said in surprise.
"Mr. Randall Montgomery is searching for his
brother."

"He'll not find him in the Hall," said the cook,
hurriedly dusting the flour from her hands and removing her apron.

"What do you mean, Mrs. McGrundy? Do you
know where he is?"

The cook nodded grimly. "I would have said
something sooner had I realized he was the one
that had hurt Mr. Westbrook!" she exclaimed, laying down her apron and starting for the passageway
leading from the kitchen.

"But where is he, Mrs. McGrundy, and where are
you going?" cried Ivy.

"I'm going to get my Sam," replied the cook.
"The young man has gone to the stables."

"To the stables?" repeated Ivy. "Why should he go
to the stables?"

"I was wondering that myself, miss, when he hadn't
ever gone before and there was nobody else out
there, Sam and his men having come in for the play."

"How strange!" said Ivy. "Edmund has no reason
to go to the stable, particularly when he will find no
one there."

"Well, there's someone else out there now!"
replied the cook. "Mr. Westbrook went out there
not five minutes ago."

Ivy stared at her in dismay. "I thought I could get

here in time to prevent him from going! What was he thinking of to go out into the storm?"

"I asked him, miss, but he told me it was nothing but a scratch and he must see to his mount. Then when I told him the other young man had just gone out, Mr. Westbrook said that that settled it. He had to go out there. And off he went."

"Was he wearing his greatcoat?" demanded Ivy. "He hadn't time to go upstairs to fetch it."

Mrs. McGrundy shook her head. "He borrowed my Sam's coat and told me he'd be back soon enough. He told me to have his mug of cider ready for him."

Ivy's knees were weak and she had some trouble keeping up with Mrs. McGrundy, who surged down the passageways toward the yellow saloon. Having caught their excitement, MacTavish led the way, looking back to bark his encouragement whenever they fell too far behind him.

Twenty

Their news set everyone in the saloon into motion. Sterling, followed closely by Gerald and Sam, rushed toward the kitchen, the rest streaming behind them. The sound of so much confusion drew Randall Montgomery back from his search for his brother.

Seeing him coming down the stairway, Ivy hurried over to him and clutched his arm.

"What is it, Miss Sterling?" he asked her. "What has happened?

"Mr. Westbrook and your brother are together in the stable, sir—and they are alone!"

Mr. Montgomery paled, but he said calmly, "Show me how I may get there, Miss Sterling. I must try to put a stop to this."

Together they hurried after the others. As they crowded into the kitchen, the back door flew open and Sam appeared, already well coated with snow, holding a length of rope in his hand.

"What is it, Sam? Why are you back so soon?" demanded Mr. Sterling.

"There's no rope to get to the stable," said Sam grimly. "It's been cut!"

"Cut?" gasped the others, staring at one another.

He nodded, holding up the rope he had in his hand. "This is all that's left of the rope that led to the stable."

"Why ever would it have been cut?" asked Ivy. "That doesn't make sense."

"Maybe the young man did it, miss," ventured Gerald. "Mrs. McGrundy says Mr. Westbrook was the second one out the door."

"But Mr. Westbrook would have turned around and come right back in, just as Sam did, if the rope had been cut," protested Ivy.

Suddenly Mrs. McGrundy rounded upon Mr. Sneed. "I'll wager it was you, Mr. Sneak!" she exclaimed. "You come along in here just behind Mr. Westbrook, and you did just what you always do in here! You opened the door and stared out a bit, then looked around the room as though you were looking for something that would fit into your pocket, and then you sneaked away just before Miss Sterling come in here!"

"That's ridiculous!" protested Mr. Sneed. "Why would I do such a thing?"

"Whether he did or whether he didn't doesn't make any difference just now," said Randall Montgomery. "We need to get to the stable. If Mr. Westbrook and my brother come to blows, Mr. Westbrook will be further injured. We must find them directly."

There was a murmur of agreement, and Gerald ran to get the length of rope that they had pieced together for Westbrook's trip to the gatehouse.

After he had secured it firmly, Randall Montgomery and Alistair Sterling struggled through the storm, led by Sam McGrundy and followed by Mr. Jarvis, who insisted upon going along.

The group in the kitchen waited anxiously, but they knew it would take several attempts for the men to find their way through the storm. The only comfort they had was that at least the rescue party could not lose their way. They had the rope.

Mrs. McGrundy had returned to her work, taking out her frustrations upon the lemons on the cutting board and grinding the coffee beans with fervor. Now and then she glanced toward Mr. Sneed, who quailed visibly. Although nothing more had been said to that gentleman, he was hemmed in by Gerald and two of the other footmen, all sturdy young men.

When the door opened again, everyone looked up eagerly, but Sam shook his head as they entered. The four men were accompanied only by Edmund Montgomery.

"Where is Mr. Westbrook?" cried Ivy. "Was he too weak to make the trip back?"

Sam shook his head again, but he waited for his master to speak. "I'm afraid Mr. Westbrook never made it to the stable," said Alistair Sterling.

Ivy sank down on the settle, and MacTavish moved protectively to her side. "But what could have happened?" she asked. "Do you suppose he fainted from exertion and loss of blood, as Miss Durrell said he might?"

"It's possible," conceded her uncle, "but there was another problem, too."

"Another problem? What was the other problem?" she demanded.

Sterling stared grimly at Edmund Montgomery, who looked away from him. "It appears once Mr. Montgomery reached the warmth and safety of the stable, he decided to cut the rope at his end so that he could maintain his privacy for a while."

For a moment there was silence in the room, and then a hubbub broke out as the truth dawned upon them. Mr. Sneed, looking wildly at those about him, turned pale and shook his head.

"Here now!" he exclaimed. "How was I to know Montgomery was going to do such a thing?" he asked. "I wasn't trying to kill Westbrook—just have him away from the Hall for a bit."

Ivy was sitting with the back of her hand pressed to her mouth, but she suddenly rose and walked toward the door.

"We have to find him! He is out there wandering in the storm with no idea of which direction to take! He could have gone in any direction—or he could have just collapsed!"

There was a sudden flurry of activity as everyone young enough to face the storm hurried off for clothes warm enough to do so. Ivy placed MacTavish on a lead and tied it around her wrist so that her hands would be free, and as they opened the door to go out again, she said, "We shall form a human chain and we will call him. Perhaps we can be heard over the wind."

Picking up her idea, her uncle nodded, saying, "As we go out the door, we will swing as far as possible in a straight line to the west, and then I will swing the end of the line north toward the stable, like the hands of a clock moving from nine to twelve. If we haven't found him by the time we reach the new rope Sam stretched out to the stable, we will continue moving toward three o'clock, which is the east wall past the kitchen door."

"Walk carefully," instructed Jarvis. "If he's fallen, we don't wish to step on him."

"What if he's gone farther than that?" demanded one of the footmen.

Gerald glared at him. "Then we'll try something else," he retorted. "Let's go!"

The line plunged out into the storm, some thirty strong. Everyone had come, except for Wheeling and Mrs. McGrundy, and everyone was calling for Westbrook. Moved by the noise, MacTavish contributed his bit by sudden bursts of sharp barking. The cold was piercing, but they continued patiently on, holding one another's hands and stretching out their line so that, like the hand of that clock, they crept slowly toward ten o'clock, then toward eleven.

Ivy paced with slow determination, calling Mr. Westbrook's name and stepping carefully for fear she was about to put her foot down upon him. Ahead of her, MacTavish patiently plowed through the drifts. Carefully she kept herself from thinking they might not find him. They would, of course, discover him and take him into the kitchen and safety. She could not allow herself to think otherwise.

For just an instant, she imagined she would not

hear his voice again, nor hear his maddening, teasing remarks. A sudden stab of loss made her realize just how deeply she would miss him. That she would not see him again was unthinkable, and she firmly closed the door on that possibility. She had to do something more, she told herself, wondering just what it could be.

She was linked between Miss Durrell and Mr. Jarvis. "I must go farther down the line—to the end of it!" she called to Jarvis. "Can you help me?"

Jarvis nodded, and taking her arm, moved her in front of him to his left side and took Miss Durrell's hand. Calling to Gerald, who was to his left, he said, "Pass Miss Sterling along! She's going to the end of the line!"

And so she made it to the very end, where she allowed MacTavish to bob about beyond the end of the line, burrowing through drifts and barking. Just as the line had passed the rope strung from Hall to stable and had swung down toward two o'clock, Ivy heard a sudden shout, and she felt the tug of the lead on her wrist as MacTavish went wild with leaping.

Through the snow emerged a dark form with the terrier under his arm. "You appear to be a part of the package, Miss Sterling," he gasped, following the lead and taking the arm she extended to him. Held between Ivy and her uncle, they were passed down the line to the safety of the kitchen door, and the rest of the frozen group flocked into the kitchen behind them.

"God be praised!" called Mrs. McGrundy as they

staggered through the door and helped Westbrook to the settle. Like Ivy, she had not allowed herself to think they might not be successful in their rescue effort, and she had worked steadily, preparing hot food and cider by the quart, praying as she worked.

She deftly removed Sam's coat from Westbrook's shoulders as Gerald used a bootjack to remove his tall leather boots. Mrs. McGrundy had placed heavy socks and a blanket to warm before the fire, and Gerald slipped the socks on Westbrook's feet and placed the blanket over his lap. While Mrs. McGrundy dried his hair and smoothed it back, Ivy was kneeling in front of the fire, drying MacTavish.

"I say, Mrs. McGrundy," Westbrook gasped, "the towel you're using on my hair doesn't belong to the little beast, does it?"

The cook laughed. "No, sir. This one is quite fresh."

Westbrook eyed the dog, who returned the earnest gaze. "Well, I suppose even if it was the little beast's towel, I wouldn't mind sharing it now. After all, he found me."

"So he did," said Ivy proudly, patting her dog on the head. "He did a very good job."

"And so did you, Ivy," remarked her uncle. Then he turned to his guest. "My niece had us form the chain to search for you, sir. And she insisted upon putting herself and her dog on the very end of it."

"Indeed?" said Westbrook, beginning to revive as Mrs. McGrundy placed a mug of hot cider in his hand. "I am most grateful, Miss Sterling—and most surprised, I must confess. As I told you, I had always suspected you would be the one to cut the rope on me."

At the mention of the rope, Edmund Montgomery and Mr. Sneed both looked acutely uncomfortable.

"I did not intend to cut you loose, Westbrook," said Edmund stiffly. "If you had come out to the stable, I would have been glad enough to finish our quarrel."

"Hopefully in a more honorable way than you did by attacking him onstage," said Miss Durrell briskly. "And, speaking of that, Mr. Westbrook, how is your wound? Did you damage it in your adventure?"

Westbrook shook his head and grinned. "There will be no more bleeding, for I'm certain that the blood has frozen solid."

The ladies in the group shuddered, and Edmund Montgomery had the grace to look ashamed.

"I believe, Mr. Westbrook, I must offer my brother's apologies to you and to the rest of this party," said Randall Montgomery, bowing. "If you will excuse us, I believe it would be best if we went upstairs now and remained apart from you and the others. I give you my word we will depart as soon as the weather will allow."

And bowing to his host, he led his younger brother from the room.

"Here now, Mr. Westbrook," said Sneed uneasily. "I cut the rope on this end, and I knew you was on it, but I never knew that the rope had been cut at the other end as well."

Westbrook eyed him speculatively, as did the rest

of the group. The others had divested themselves
of their coats and scarves and gloves and boots, and
the kitchen smelled strongly of wet wool, cider, baking meat pies, and the spices for mulled wine, for
Mrs. McGrundy was preparing a celebratory drink
in honor of the rescue. It seemed to Sneed as
though the crowd was drawing dangerously close
about him, and he shivered a little.

"But, Mr. Sneed," said Westbrook reasonably, "why
would you wish to cut the rope at all? Had I said
something to you that you particularly disliked?"

Sneed shook his head desperately, but it did not
appear he was going to explain himself any further.

"I think I'll just step upstairs, Sneed, and have a
look through your gear," said Jarvis suddenly, looking down coldly at the little man.

"Look through my gear?" repeated Sneed nervously. "There's no need for that, is there?"

"I believe there is," said Jarvis. "I'd noticed you
stowing away some things there, and if I ain't
greatly mistook, I'm thinking there'll be a silver
spoon or two among them."

"Aha!" exclaimed Mrs. McGrundy triumphantly
to Ivy. "What did I tell you, miss? And it won't be
one or two spoons—it'll be a round dozen of
them!"

Mr. Ravensby stared at Mr. Sneed with repug-
nance, and he drew himself up to his full
pigeon-chested best. "I cannot believe, sir, that you
would so sully the reputation of our troupe. Go
immediately to his chamber, Mr. Jarvis, and bring
the purloined spoons here."

Jarvis departed immediately, and Sneed collapsed in a corner, staring disconsolately at the others. When Jarvis returned, he had in hand the missing spoons, as well as Ivy's jeweled miniature of her mother and a diamond stickpin belonging to Mr. Sterling.

"And so, Mr. Sneed, you simply wished to have me out of the way for a while so you could shop through my belongings for anything you might wish to add to your collection," observed Westbrook. "I must say your timing was remarkably poor, unless you wished to find yourself in the hangman's noose."

Sneed shuddered visibly at this ominous reference and put his head in his hands. Mr. Ravensby then turned to his host.

"Pray accept my profound apologies, Mr. Sterling," he said with feeling. "To think you took us in out of the cold and we have repaid you so shabbily! I shudder to consider what you must think of us."

"Nonsense, Mr. Ravensby," replied Alistair Sterling, slipping his arm inconspicuously around Miss Durrell's waist. "Your coming to my home has been a blessing I will thank you for all the days of my life."

Mr. Ravensby's chest grew even fuller at this praise. "I have prided myself upon the abilities of my troupe," he said, "but never has our work been lauded so warmly. I am overcome! Words fail me!"

Ivy, having had some experience with Mr. Ravensby, was certain this was far from being true. As he continued his oration to her uncle, she turned to Mr. Westbrook and smiled, then seated

herself next to him on the settle. Westbrook spread
the blanket over her lap as well and put his arm
around her shoulders.

"Well, Miss Sterling?" he whispered. "I warned
you I would be asking you again. What do you say
to becoming Mrs. Robert Westbrook so you can
keep me in proper order? Do you feel equal to the
task?"

She looked at him dubiously. "Well, I don't know,
sir. That would be a most difficult undertaking."

A sudden tugging at the blanket caught their attention. Its folds spilled onto the stone floor, and
MacTavish was circling there, making a comfortable nest for himself.

"But you would have help," he reminded her,
pointing at the dog. "Don't forget the small beast."

She nodded, smiling. "He would be helpful, of
course."

"Perhaps you may wish to marry at the end of the
season, Miss Sterling?" he asked. "After your coming out? I understand June weddings are very
fashionable."

"I believe I would enjoy being fashionable," she
admitted, dimpling as he bent down to kiss her.

Mr. Ravensby was still holding forth about the
merits of his troupe, but Alistair Sterling glanced
down at Miss Durrell, and they both looked over
at Ivy and Westbrook and smiled.

"I do so like happy endings," murmured Miss
Durrell, putting her head on Alistair's shoulder.

Epilogue

"Well, it is a fine day, don't you think, Jarvis?" inquired Robert Westbrook, walking briskly toward his carriage.

"It is indeed, sir," agreed Jarvis, opening the carriage door for his master. "We have a good day for our journey."

"Are you and your wife quite prepared?" inquired Westbrook.

Jarvis nodded, grinning. "Betty has packed our belongings twice over, sir. She is that excited about going back to Foxridge Hall to visit."

The front door of the Westbrook house opened and Ivy came hurrying down the steps, followed by MacTavish and two small boys.

"Oh, do be careful, Alistair," she cautioned the elder one as he attempted to leap to the pavement from the top of the steps. "If you skin your knee before we leave, we shall have to stop and doctor it, then we will not make it to your uncle and aunt's before midnight tonight."

"I am careful, Mama," he called reassuringly. "I can do it with no difficulty." And here he leaped from the top step, landing neatly upon his feet. "Will I be able to fence with Aunt Divina when we arrive?"

"I am certain she will be delighted to fence with you," Ivy reassured him. "Now come along, Alistair, and help your brother Leigh down the steps so that he doesn't fall."

Soon the group was packed into the carriage, and Jarvis joined Betty and the other servants in the coach that would follow them. Briskly, the party set out for Foxridge Hall, where Gerald would open the door for them, Uncle Alistair and Aunt Divina would be waiting, and Mrs. McGrundy would have prepared all of their favorite foods, including porridge for MacTavish.

It was, Ivy thought, smiling to herself, the way life should be. As though on cue, MacTavish looked up at her and barked, wagging his tail in agreement.

ABOUT THE AUTHOR

MONA GEDNEY lives with her family in Indiana and is the author of twelve Zebra Regency romances and is working on her next, FROST FAIR FIANCÉ, to be published in May 2003. Mona loves to hear from readers, and you may write to her c/o Zebra Books. Please include a self-addressed stamped envelope if you wish a response.